THE IMPASSE

Praise for Franci McMahon

Night Mare

"Ms. McMahon knows her stuff, and writes flawlessly...She also tells a whale of a tale. An excellent, two-thumbs-up read." —*Midwest Book Review*

"Wow! This is one rip snorting, page turning, and exciting mystery. Even if you don't adore horses, you just have to cringe at some of the things that are done to them just for money, but our heroine Jane Scott is going to get the evildoers even if it involves danger to her own body...I sure hope to see more stories by this writer, as she is exceptionally adept in storytelling as well as character development."—*Golden Threads Newsletter*

"*Night Mare* is the type of book you're really sorry to see end!...This is a beautifully written book...You'll like Jane, and this mystery, whether or not you're a lover of horses!"—*Mega Scene*

"With *Night Mare*, Franci McMahon has accomplished a difficult feat. She has written a mystery that will appeal to readers who don't read mysteries. And she has achieved this through an original plot and strong characters...Franci McMahon has a gift for character development and a way of engaging readers that makes *Night Mare* a truly worthwhile read."—*Sacred Ground: Reviews and News on Lesbian Writing*

"[A]n entertaining read, the lesbians are not all 'good,' the straight folk aren't all anti-gay bigots, and I learned something about the economics of horses."—*Out in the Mountains*

Staying the Distance

"This first novel is a thoroughly escapist adventure and romance on horseback…McMahon writes the love scenes convincingly and sensitively, and she beautifully describes the Montana landscape… An enjoyable book, particularly for horse enthusiasts, that belongs in public libraries."—*Library Journal*

"Cowgirls, take a break from two-stepping, hop on the steed of your dreams, and come for a good long gallop. Rachel Duncan, who owns her own spread in Montana and raises Arabian horses, is training for the Tevis Cup, the 'toughest horse race of all,' one hundred miles in one day through mountain country. In short, this tall, gangly gal wearing Western boots and leather chaps is every cowgirl's dream…Whether the reader cares about horses or not, Rachel's intensity about them makes the book exciting…Like Rachel's Arabian horses, this story is sensible, hardy, and smart." —*Lambda Book Report*

"*Staying the Distance* is really a good book. I enjoyed it a whole lot and learned more about horses than I'll probably ever have cause to use. McMahon has a real eye for just the right detail…She, like her heroine, tackles issues head-on, and the result is delightful." —*Bay Windows*

By the Author

Staying the Distance

Night Mare

White Horse in Winter

The Impasse

THE IMPASSE

by

Franci McMahon

2017

THE IMPASSE

ISBN 13: 978-1-62639-781-1

This Trade Paperback Original Is Published By
Bold Strokes Books, Inc.
P.O. Box 249
Valley Falls, NY 12185

First Edition: February 2017

CREDITS
EDITOR: JERRY L. WHEELER
PRODUCTION DESIGN: STACIA SEAMAN
COVER PHOTO OF CHINESE WALL: FRANCI MCMAHON
COVER DESIGN BY MELODY POND

Acknowledgments

I am very fortunate to have some excellent readers and critiques for *The Impasse*. I found Laney Webber among the beta readers at the Golden Crown Literary Society. Her comments were pure gold, and I cannot thank her enough for her concise comments as well as her enthusiasm. And to the woman who has looked many mountain wildfires in the face, I'd like to thank Cheryl Martin for vetting my fictional fire. Thank you to my friend in Australia, rescuer of kangaroos, sister of the malt, and fellow author at Bold Strokes Books, Mardi Alexander, for being an early reader of the manuscript. Thanks to Carsen Taite for the book in my kit. My deepest appreciation goes to my editor Jerry Wheeler and all the talented people at Bold Strokes Books.

for Jenifer Wise

CHAPTER ONE

Over a year has gone by since Jane died. Isn't that what it's supposed to take? A year of mourning. Each day I struggle to stay functional and tackle the jobs that must be done around the ranch. When I returned home from Vermont three days after Jane's death, I had gathered cows from the high mountain grazing, just as I had every other year of my life. I have no memory of that year's cattle drive down to winter pasture. This fall, my heart isn't filled with lead. It's too shriveled up and dry to have any weight.

Black Angus cows flow like a creek downhill, standing out against the bright sun-yellowed October grass. Back in the spring, when we drove them from the valley to the summer grass in the high parks, the calves were young, their mothers worried, constantly calling. They move silently now that their calves have grown independent. Soon most of them will be sold, carried away by cattle trucks.

Most people love the fall, that time of slow transition to winter and rest, but I knew those cows would bawl for their calves day and night. That sound always ripped me apart. I think I'm too raw this year.

I yell to my brother, "Norburt, I'll ride ahead and get the gate."

"Okay, Sis." The brim of his hat dips. He taps his thigh, says, "Myrna, here! That'll do, Skip."

Myrna comes to the side of his horse, watching Burt for the next thing he wants from her. She is classic Blue Heeler, driven to herd. Skipper, a blue merle Border collie, drops to the ground, eyeing the cows' slow shuffle toward the corner gate. I'd had to leave Scout at home because Jane's terrier gets too excited around the cows, chasing them in all directions.

Burt takes his wide-brimmed hat off to wipe his forehead with his bright red bandanna, and then he sweeps his sandy hair back and settles his hat in place. He's overdue for a haircut.

I lift my reins and ask my horse to jog up to the barbed wire gate, which I unfasten from the saddle and drag open to hook the top wire on a fence post. My buckskin mare, named, of course, Buck, is patient while I count the cows passing between the gateposts.

Burt knows his job is not to bunch them up, but let them string out.

"Forty-three," I call out. All cows accounted for. Should be the same number of calves, if the wolves or lions didn't pick out an easy dinner. Three bulls. They are the worst to gather, not being social like the cows. They go off by themselves and get missed in the roundup.

This gather brings cows to a total herd of one hundred fifty-one. Nine registered Angus bulls. I think about my three grazing allotments, and the number of cows I'm allowed to graze each year by the BLM and Forest Service. With all the money Jane left me, things aren't so tight. Before, in a bad year of stillborn calves or barren cows, I'd have pitiful small reserves to fall back on.

I notice the grass is a little short. Mid-August, three months ago, was the last time I packed the two fifty-pound blocks of salt up to Hadley Park. At the time I thought the grazing would hold up better. Not enough rain, I expect.

In the interest of taking some pressure off the grassland, I'll sell off twenty of my good producing cows to another rancher. I'm considering not selling the calves this year, instead transitioning to an organic grass-fed beef market.

I bite the fingers of my glove to pull it off, then reach down and undo the snap at the waist of my Levis. *Well, Miles, your damn pants are getting too tight. Oh, yeah. Slacking off on the work, more like. Or handing too much off to Burt. Or eating too much. Better than drinking. But then maybe some of that, too.*

After Burt and the dogs follow the cows through, I come along, leaving the gate open for the elk and any strays from other ranches working their way out of the mountains when the snow hits. I look around. Won't be long now. Last month, the aspen were bright as molten gold flowing off the fir-covered hills. Now the trees are lacy bare black against the blue sky, framing the burning scarlet of the red twig dogwood in the lower drainages.

From here, I can see the valley where the ranch holds our land to the earth. The grass is winter yellow, cured by the hot sun and lack of rain.

I close my eyes and breathe out slowly. I'm dreading the long winter ahead.

❖

Three weeks after a dreary Christmas where Burt and I were snowbound for a week, I'm in the kitchen trying to find some after-dinner snack. Wind rattles the windows with such a racket I have to walk up to the door to make out if it is a person knocking. "Someone there?"

I'm shocked to my toes to actually hear a voice answer. Visitors are rare in January. I kick the draft dodger to one side and pull the door open. Scout barks. Skipper stands stiff and alert.

Standing on the small covered porch is a tall woman in a green hooded parka. Her hunched back is to the wind, which is driving snow in hard-packed ridges across the yard.

"Miles?" She turns and faces me. I like her face, winnowed like the snow.

I pull the door wide. "Come on in. Get back, Scout, and be quiet."

Striding through the door, she shakes the hood back to show a crown of short white hair. Her face, with warm brindle brown eyes, is loaded with character and a centeredness not seen in most people. "Karen Smyth. I called last week about meeting with you, remember? Right after the new year?"

"Sure," I lie. Her accent spoke of far-off New England and gives me a jolt. "Come on into the living room by the fire. How about coffee? Or tea?"

She nods and whispers, "Tea. Thank you, Ms. Miles."

"Just Miles will do well enough." I fill and plug in the electric kettle, then lead her into the living room and crank up the gas fireplace. Karen peels off her parka, and I drape it over a chair near the heater. The dogs follow us into the living room to sniff her ankles, coat, and the air around her. Karen offers her hand to the dog noses. She leans forward to spread her hands close to the fire. "Gets as cold as this in Maine, but the wind...oh, my! Cuts through you like a knife."

I nod, stand up, and push the curtain back to see the thermometer. "It's only twenty below."

"Is that all?" Her voice has a playful edge about it. She's one of those lean, bony types that feel the cold.

"Why not take your boots off. I've got some rabbit fur slippers you could wear."

Karen flinches when I say "rabbit," and I realize I've got an animal rights activist in my living room. I can't remember why she's come to see me. Maybe to convince me to not raise beef cows.

"I've got some wool ones, too. The sheep didn't die in the making of them." I laugh to show her no hard feelings.

She looks me square and gives me a winter-thawing smile. "Perfect." She's working at the frozen bootlaces as I fetch her next footwear.

On the way back, I bring two mugs of chamomile tea and sugar, and I shove the slippers in my armpit. Once we're all cozy and comfortable, I wait for her to tell me why she's sitting in my brown chair in Montana in the thick of winter.

I stretch my legs out toward the fire, noticing too late I'm wearing my rough out elk hide slippers. Oh, hell. Not something I can worry about.

"I can't remember..." Karen starts out slowly.

I'm stuck back on her Maine accent, "cawnt."

"...how much background I gave you. My outdoor travel business is called Her Wilderness, and I lead backcountry trips for women. All of my treks strive for the connection of spirit and nature, an interior voyage as well as the physical. I'm a licensed Maine Guide, so most of my journeys involve water and take place in Maine. Women began requesting other trips; a journaling one set in Utah's Escalante, or a watercolor-painting excursion down the Green River. Well, lately I've had many inquiries about Montana's Chinese Wall in the Bob Marshall Wilderness. I hear it is one of the world's most impressive natural uplifts."

"You bet. The wall is a sheer drop of a thousand feet,

extending north and south for twenty or so miles. It runs as a spine down the center of the area, actually the Continental Divide. Hard to get to because it is a wilderness, so no motorized vehicles are allowed."

"That's what I understand. Only the most rugged backpackers venture into those mountains. I gather the best way to travel is by horseback with an outfitter who packs in everything. I decided that would make the most sense for a women's trip, so I asked around. Your name arose as being familiar with that country."

"I'm no outfitter, but yes, I've been back to the Wall. A few times." I gazed at the gas flames and flashed back to my first love, Ginger, whose parents owned an outfitting business. We rode with them many summers just so we could be together, up until her horse took a wrong step and ended up three hundred feet down on the creek bedrocks. Mostly on top of her.

Karen had grown silent. I looked over to her. "Guess I took a little trip."

"To a hard place, I gather."

I nod once. "Go on."

"The plan is to take eight guests on horseback."

"Eight. From what I understand, most outfitters consider nine or ten to be the minimum for profit. Isn't that going to cut you short on all the expenses?"

"I've spoken with a few outfitters, and that's what they all say. However, women will pay a premium to have an all-women experience. Eight is a more manageable number."

"Karen, I don't have the stock or the equipment to run that sort of adventure."

"Actually, I got your name from Jess Montgomery out of Wyoming. She is well-equipped but has never been into the Bob Marshall Wilderness."

"Oh, yeah. Jess. I remember she did some outfitting work for a party I took on a cattle drive. Nice folks. They wanted to see the backcountry in Yellowstone, and I sent them to her. Good reputation, but I've never met her."

I stare at the fire again, doing some calculations. "So she can supply seventeen or eighteen head of stock, horses and mules, a wrangler, and all the fixings to the jump-off point?" I feel creeping up a rising excitement, an enthusiasm for life I haven't felt in a long time. This plan could be a kick, something to look forward to.

"Oh, no problem, Miles. She assures me she has trained, gentle animals and experienced staff."

"We'll need eleven riding horses and six pack animals. I'll bring my own horse. This isn't a trot on bridle trails, you know. There are drop-offs along the trail that'll make you sick to your stomach. There's one place to put up wall tents on a Forest Service outfitter lease site. I know the outfitter who runs that camp, just on the far side of the wilderness boundary. That's twenty-four miles in. A long day's ride. Will the women on this trip at least know how to ride?"

Karen's face stills. "I hadn't thought about that…just assumed."

"I'd stress in your advertising that women who want to go should take riding lessons, two hours a week for a couple of months beforehand. Even if they learned how to ride back when they were twelve, they need to wake those muscles up and get over the initial pain-when-climbing-stairs stage."

"I rode as a child, in shows."

"Right." I look at her doubtfully. "We need a head and heel on both the strings, dude and pack. I can head the pack animals with a rider to tail, but we'll need someone who can handle horses and emergencies in two more positions. Jess can lead the dudes. You could tail if you can brush up on your skills."

"I gather you are on board," Karen says, her brown eyes bright.

"Wouldn't miss it for the world."

Chapter Two

I talk Karen into staying in the spare bedroom. The drive back to Bozeman to find a motel would be too far in the wind and dark. Before I turn in, I take an extension cord out to her rental car and plug in the block heater.

In the morning, I drink a strong cup of coffee while she does her Buddhist thing. I can hear soft humming sounds coming from the bedroom down the hall. When Norburt comes in at first light for breakfast, he stands still as a rabbit trying to sort the sounds out.

"A lady came by last night after you'd gone to the bunkhouse. Wants me to do a job for her sometime this summer."

"Why's she making those noises?"

"It's a religious thing, Burt."

"Oh." He pulls a chair out and sits at the table.

"Two eggs over easy, or scrambled?"

"Bacon? Home fries?"

"No," I say. "This is winter, and we're not working so hard. Just eggs and toast. You can have your choice of canned peaches or pears."

"Scrambled with peaches, I guess."

My brother is a big breakfast eater, but the broader

concepts of life pass him by. He's been slow since birth, went to school at the Montana Developmental Center, luckily right down the road in our little county seat of Boulder. It's a residential school, so he learned a lot of "life skills" there. And way out here on the ranch with no one around, he needed the socialization.

Once I was old enough to drive, I'd go get him every weekend. He was always ready when I arrived.

I had an older brother without the ranching gene. He did, however, get the alcoholic gene, drove drunk off MacDonald Pass and killed himself. My parents bought a condo in Tucson after their cherished son's death and turned the ranch over to me to run.

Norburt had ranching in his blood, like me. And my folks considered him a non-person, like me. The two greatest disappointments of my parents' lives: a lesbian daughter and a retarded son. We had always been the only ones who wanted the ranch. He's thirty now and the hero of his schoolmates because he lives by himself in the bunkhouse, has a dog and a horse, and is a cowboy. I couldn't run the ranch without his help.

Karen enters the kitchen looking serene and centered. I smile at her and say, "Sit and have something to eat. This is my brother, Norburt. Burt, this is Karen Smyth. She lives in Maine."

Burt sits up straighter than his usual ramrod. "Pleased to meet you, ma'am. Is that where the lobsters come from?"

My jaw drops. *Where did he get that from?*

"Why yes, Norburt." Karen smoothly draws a chair out and sits across from him. She gives me one of her 100-watt smiles. "That was perfect, staying in your cozy guest bedroom. Thank you for your hospitality."

I'd like to be more sophisticated, but I blush anyway. Once breakfast is squared away, we get back to business. Norburt takes the tractor out to feed, unrolling a half-ton round bale in a long path which rapidly gets speckled with black and brown cows. Karen follows me out to feed chickens. I don't bother to look for eggs, the short days being so cold.

"Don't you use horses on your ranch?" Karen says, doubt flashing across her face. "I see your four wheeler, but…"

I smile, knowing she is worried about a rancher with no horses, especially in view of the recent job offer. "They're all out on winter pasture except three: a young horse I'll calve on who needs some higher education, a yearling, and an old retired fellow."

Karen looks around vaguely, taking in the wind whistling through sagebrush, snow hammered in ridges on the lee side, the dark firs blanketing the mountains all around. "You mean horses living out there on their own? No warm barn?"

"It's their time to pretend they're wild horses. They shelter in the trees, paw through snow to get at the grass, or the wind clears their feed for them. If it is a deep snow year, I roll some hay out. In the spring, they come in all snorty and fat." I walk to the barn. "Come on, you can meet the ones living in luxury."

Out of the wind, the barn holds what passes for warmth, the scent of sweet wheat straw and alfalfa hay. We walk down the aisle to two large stalls opening out to corrals. I throw hay into each of the built-in pole feeders along the wall and dump a scoop of molasses-laced oats and corn into corner buckets. By this time, furry beasts enter from the corral, hooves rustling through wheat straw, to nose and bang in the buckets. Crunching sounds make a trio sonata, and smoky breath rises from the buckets, turning their whiskers white.

"Don't you use blankets?" Karen eyes the horses, one a

black yearling and the other an old white gelding. The sorrel is in the second stall.

"They grow their own fur coats. I make sure they get enough calories to keep warm from the inside."

When they have finished the grain, the black filly comes up to me. I take off my gloves and scratch her under the barrel. "This one is out of a purebred Arabian who came here as a rescue horse. Some damn breeder who went belly up cut his losses by not feeding them. The mare, Alec, was in a bad way and turned out she was pregnant to boot."

I remembered back to the night she was born. I'd just returned from Vermont, reeling from the loss of Jane. Both the mare and her foal might have died if I hadn't been around to help the mare, too weak to do it on her own.

The filly nuzzled Karen. "Oh, she's looking for treats."

"No. I don't give them any hand treats. She just likes you."

Karen turns to the white horse, dark eyes watching us, nose resting on the filly's back. "And this boy? Why did you say he's here?"

"He's retired. Was a great rope horse in his day. He's taken a shine to this girl and doesn't let her out of his sight. This filly was small when she was born, not enough prenatal nutrition. When I weaned her this fall, I wanted her to be with a friend. He's a babysitter. Besides, they both need the extra feed."

"Oh," she says, rubbing the old fellow's ears. Karen turns to look at the horse in the adjacent stall. "And this one?"

"A five-year-old gelding I'll calve on next month. He needs some boring work where he slows down and waits for me."

"What's calving?"

"Late February, the cows start dropping their calves. I need to separate out the heavies and bring them in close by so

I can watch them, help them if they get into trouble calving. When the cows are turned out in the pasture with their new calves, I need to ride through the herd and make sure everyone is all right. A lot of standing around and watching for slow calves or tight udders is good for a young horse."

"Will your brother be able to manage with you away on the trip?"

"Oh, sure. If I have to be gone, I get someone to stay at the ranch. My cousin, Tess, usually can come and stay, and Burt thinks the world of her. Let's have another cup of coffee and work out a few details."

We shed our outdoor clothes in the kitchen. I turn the little gas stove up, so the flames show. I'd discovered these heaters when I was in Vermont. Now the kitchen is welcoming and warm. I put the electric kettle on.

"I'll give you Jess's email," she says.

"Better give me her phone number, too. I don't have a computer."

"Oh? Really? Guess I'm naive enough to think everyone has one."

"Don't have a cell phone, either. I'm not backward, but we don't get any reception in this high valley, miles from any tower. No TV, either. Kind of the dark ages." I laugh. "If I must get on the cyberspace mode, I can go to the library in town and use one of theirs."

We sit down with something hot to drink. "When you have a date for your trip, I'll go in with Jess and some pack animals to set up the wall tents. There's a big cook tent, which is left standing for outfitter use until after hunting season. We'll need three more for the guests. Lay in some canned and dry food. If we can do all this a few days ahead, that'll make a shorter string for the actual trip."

"Sounds good. I'll leave all those details to Jess and you. The food should be all vegetarian. Will that be difficult?"

"No. I prefer it actually. Less aromas to attract the bears."

Karen lowers her eyebrows. "Are grizzlies a problem? Will it be dangerous? We have black bear in Maine, but…do I need to worry about…?"

"Grizzlies have never attacked a group of over six people. I like to be aware of reducing activities that draw them to camp. Cooking meat is one of those. You must have some good meal plans from other trips. If you'd like, why not send me a menu with a list of ingredients and snacks? Include an idea of what the budget will be."

"I can do that. And I have a great sprout-growing setup."

"Always good to have fresh greens. I'll pick up a selection of seeds. Helena has a good health food store. We'll need a separate list of fresh food for Jess to pick up on her way hauling up the riding horses."

"When do you think would be good to plan weather-wise?"

"Weather's changeable in the Bob. Early July would be late enough. Most of the snow's off, and you run into fire season if you go too late. By the end of September, snow can once again be a problem."

"Short window for trips." Karen studies me over her coffee mug.

"As soon as you have some idea of the date, let me know so I can set things up here. The camp needs to be booked with the outfitters. Also, when you have the guest list firmed up, I'd like to check it out. Get a fix on their equine backgrounds and abilities. I have a terrible time with names, and that'll shorten the learning curve."

"Yes, I'll send you copies of the applications."

Karen suggests the budgeted payment for me to guide the

group, and I tell her that is fine. If she only knew, I'd do it for nothing.

We grip each other's hands in a satisfying shake, and I walk her out to her rented car. I unplug the block heater and stand there holding the plug, then raise my arm to send her off.

I am sad to see her go. Not many women drop in for a visit, especially one who brings an adventure to plan for. Back in the kitchen, I dial the number for Jess to get some early plans laid. She picks up on the third ring, "Yellowstone Horse Excursions, how can I help you?"

After I introduce myself she says, "You're the guide Karen Smyth arranged. Yes, I gave her your name. I'll send you an employment form, and I'll need three references."

Well, that sort of brings me up short. "I thought I was working for Karen."

"No. You'll be my employee. I'll be responsible for the trip."

This gal sure is rubbing me the wrong way. "Let's just call my involvement a subcontract." Before she gets stuck on that, I head on straight ahead. "We'll need to pack in about a week before the trip starts. Set up three wall tents and take the bulk of supplies. Can you have six head of stock at Benchmark by then? I'll bring my own riding horse."

The silence on the line tells me Jess is regrouping. "I can't just commit to an unknown campsite. How do I know it will be suitable?"

"Some things you'll just have to take my word for. This is the only level spot anywhere around. It's a twenty-four-mile ride from Benchmark, which is west of Augusta. The camping site isn't in the Bob, it's just outside the boundary."

"How far is it from this Chinese Wall?"

"An easy ride of an hour from the camp up to the top. It's a truly awesome sight, that wall snaking—"

She interrupts me. "So, what's at this camp for the dudes? It's my responsibility to see they are comfortable. Are there cots?"

"Those cots are like torture chambers. We can pack a dozen air mattresses for more comfort. A cook tent is set up already. The outfitters who own it remove it after hunting season. There's a spring and permanent corrals for the stock."

I can imagine her pursed lips as she emits a skeptical disapproving sound. I'm not warming up to this gal.

"Twenty-four miles of mountain riding. That's a hard ride for dudes. Seems to me we should go half the distance and camp." Jess sounds impatient.

"Complicates things too much. Tents, picket lines, food prep. And I'll be leading everyone with the pack string, so there's a danger of the riders getting lost. The best is to push through and take a day to recover in camp. If the riders can get on the trail by six in the morning, we'll get there before dark."

"I'll send someone up with horses and pack gear. I'm much too busy to make two trips, but I can spare one person. Her name is Charlene, and she's good with horses. I'll be there in time with the riding horses and the rest of the supplies."

"I'll lay in all the dry or canned food stuff. I'll email a list of the rest for you to bring up with you. Won't be much. Fresh food, like carrots and cheese."

I can tell Jess isn't very happy. Much more used to giving orders than being a team player. I cross my fingers that Charlene will be more likable.

CHAPTER THREE

The black filly had shot up during those last months of her second winter. She'd been a late foal, born in October, so though I called her a yearling, she was four months short of two years old in April. Her education so far had consisted of learning to stand when tied and being handled, walking beside me quietly, and moving away at the touch of a hand. Short travels in the horse trailer with her old friend were now old hat.

Sometimes I'd be standing there, doing something normal like watching the filly, and out of nowhere, I'd be blindsided by the vivid picture of me helping this filly into the world. Me lying on my side with my hands sorting out obstetrics chains and colt feet, holding a grief so fierce my chest felt crushed.

In those long months of that first winter of sorrow, my body moved as if powered by frozen gears instead of muscles. The first few weeks, I couldn't read. The words never came together into sentences. I couldn't listen to music without tears. I think I checked every single action movie out of the library, avoiding "happily ever afters."

During my better days, I hand tooled the saddle I was building for my cousin, Tess.

Often sleepless, I'd shake my head and run my fingers through my hair, digging into the scalp. Those were dark days and I was relieved they were getting fewer and farther between.

Today is a sunny, warm day, and spring is driving the cold and dark winter back. I can't be in the house another minute, and I figure I should do something more with that filly. I lead her into the round pen and set the saddle I used as a kid on the top pole for her to study. I had ridden it hard, and it had already been chewed a few times, little exploratory bites here and there. I leave it there for her to nose and lick, and go to breakfast.

When I come back, Burt is with me. He rests against the rails to watch the show.

I sack the filly with an old wool saddle pad, and settle it on her back when she stops flinching at the touch. As she noses the pad, I notice a few white hairs along her muzzle. I realize she will turn gray by the time she is grown. I am always partial to grays, and with the old horse's time getting short, somehow it pleases me.

I reach over to the saddle and hold it for her to check out from all angles, and then I slowly place it on her back. No fuss. After a few minutes, I do up the cinch not too tight, just enough to hold it in place. I turn and walk off. She follows me like she has worn a saddle all her life. I fuss over her, scratch her in all her favorite places, then remove the saddle and blanket.

I say to Burt as I go out the gate, "She's going gray."

"Well, I'll be. She looks black to me, Sis."

"She'll shed out gray by the time she's five, I expect. These Arabians are slow to change."

"When are you going to ride her?"

"Not until she's four."

"That long?"

"She's small, and this breed takes longer to develop." I

head for the tack room, Norburt and the dogs following. "I'll go find the horses and drive them in today. You okay on your own for lunch?"

"I'll make a sandwich. You want me to turn the filly out?"

"Leave her in the round pen until I return. She will be upset that I'm taking Whitey."

"Sure thing, Sis."

I saddle up the old man, who gets as frisky as a colt when I put my leg across him. I whistle for Skipper, but she is standing at my side, ready to go. I hear some desperate separation anxiety calls from the filly as we ride away. She has never joined up with the sorrel gelding. I left her in the round pen so she can act up without danger of getting hurt. Good for her to discover she could be without her soul mate and live through the experience. Guess it is time to name her, called her "the filly" most of the time. Midnight or Raven are just too teenage girl, and those names wouldn't work anyway now that she's turning gray. I'll come up with something.

When I ride through the section gate on the far side of the pasture, I leave it open to bring the horses through. The yellow grass meadows are greening up in the sun, but patches of snow hide in the shady places under the firs.

At the top of a rise, I can hear the old fellow breathing and let him stop to blow. While waiting for Whitey to get his breath back, I look across the valley at Bull Mountain, snow covering the hump of the summit. Douglas firs blanket the sides, reaching down to the valley grasslands. Startling red patches of beetle kill lodgepole pine mix in with the blue-green firs in higher places. I pray lightning doesn't spark them into a forest fire before they drop their needles.

I feel the old horse stiffen beneath me in alert attention. His ears point to a line of aspen following a drainage out of the hills. We go that direction and, sure enough, the horses are grazing just on the other side of the trees. Riding well to the outside of the herd of a dozen horses, we get south of them, then I send Skip out to gather.

I take a close look at the herd of eleven horses and one mule. They are in good shape, patches of winter coat shedding at their shoulders and along their sleek sides. The sorrel Arabian, Alec, is shiny and fat, fitting in with the herd and frisking with the best of them. Buck has assumed the lead mare position. She tosses her black mane and tail, shoots her ears back at one of the stragglers, and gallops along the herd's flank. Her darker winter coat is shedding, exposing her sandy buckskin color.

They set off leaping and cavorting toward home and the grain they know they'll get. The old horse has a hard time keeping up with them, and by the time I'd closed the gate, I knew I'd need to blanket him for the rest of the day. His ears are up and happy for a change in the routine.

Seeing Whitey content and having fun makes me think about myself. What sustains me? Talking with Karen brought up some old thoughts. My so-called spirituality is a rusty theory. My parents are Methodists, but I never belonged there. Always had trouble seeing how such a judgmental God of Christianity could ever speak to me, as a lesbian.

How could people buy into that crap anyway? God moves in mysterious ways. Yeah, like killing both my first love, Ginger, and just when I found someone to love, Jane. There were problems between us, sure, but I felt cheated out of the chance to work them out.

You have to laugh because the only radio stations you can get clearly on long road trips across endless miles of high plains are the Christian ones. The music sounds like they are drugged out, swooning over God and his love.

When I was with Jane, I'd been to a Quaker Friends

meeting in Vermont. I felt a strong pull to that quiet peace and respectfulness of all living things.

What Karen spoke of was something I'd always felt, a connection and awareness that I was of the earth. The only time I feel whole is when I'm immersed in natural things: standing under those big firs on the shoulder of Bull Mountain, or at the side of a rushing stream, and, of course, on the back of a horse. Not all horses. Some are too defensive and suspicious of humans, but a horse like Whitey, right there between my legs, alert, willing, and responsive.

I get off Whitey to close the gate. The horses are jockeying for position at the feeders and the grain Burt has ready for them. I mount up and Whitey shuffles toward the barns. His ears perk at the black filly's greeting neigh.

This short ride is his last.

Somehow this makes me incredibly sad. I lead him into the barn and give him a good rubdown, buckle a blanket over his damp coat, and leave him in the stall to rest.

After I close the stall door, I lean my arms across the top and dream back to the time we were young, this horse and I. He was the first horse I'd trained from a colt. When he was five and I was working the high school rodeo circuit, we were unbeatable. Every time I'd shake out my rope and back into the box, he'd take me out right next to the steer and hold steady while I dropped the loop over the steer's horns.

My dad praised the job I'd done with Whitey, and my older brother couldn't say anything good. Jack wasn't much of a horseman, but that didn't stop him from hating me for doing well. He left for college, got interested in cars, girls, and high-paying jobs. He soon disdained the hard work of the ranch, and I sighed with relief.

Norburt was another matter. He loved the ranch, and from the time he was a little kid I'd teach him whatever I could.

Found a really nice little quarter horse gelding, gentle as a kitten for him to train. Soon, we were riding together in Team Penning competitions, often with our cousin Tess.

I drop my arms and step back from the stall door. I know I'm one of the lucky ones to live this sort of life, to have this ranch to love and run. I just needed a woman to share it with.

CHAPTER FOUR

The pastures are full of frisking calves, and the hills blooming with pink shooting stars and blue bells when Karen calls to tell me her trip date. "August tenth. I have eight very eager women signed up who will arrive on the ninth. They all assure me they have riding time arranged and will be in shape for the trip. One even rides long-distance races for fun."

"Great. I'll book the camp. There's lodging in Augusta that can house us the night before." I give her the number to make reservations. "We should use the hotel the night we get off the Bob too. Everyone can fly out of Great Falls the following day."

"I sent you copies of the applications this morning. And I just got off the phone with Jess. She will send up the pack stock and a wrangler as you requested on the seventh of August. Will that work for you, Miles?"

"The fifth would be better, one day in, one day to set up, and another to ride out. One day for the stock to rest. I'll give her a call to move the date up. We're all set. I'll get it rolling."

"By the way," Karen clears her throat, "she wanted me to sign a release for you, something about not being liable for your mistakes. Since you refuse to be her employee."

I groan. "I'm calling myself a subcontractor."

A soft chuckle comes to me from Maine. "I told her that was fine with me."

❖

I make my own plans for the summer. Time to use some of that money Jane had unexpectedly left me. Those loose windows in the kitchen will be a good place to start. I call a contractor I've hired a few times, James Gray, who talks me into refitting all the windows, not just the kitchen ones. I'm so used to penny-pinching, it is hard to commit to spend anything. And I'm so used to cold hands and feet in the winter, I forget I can change that.

While I'm at it, I make arrangements to add Core-Bond insulation to the space under the roof. The contractor told me only three inches of fiberglass are up there, which in the old days was thought to be plenty.

The excursion will start before all the hay is in. Norburt would need some help with that. I ask around for a farm hand who can stay at the bunkhouse and finish the haying job. I worry about finding someone who will fit with Norburt. Most people figure he has no brains or ability to get a job done, but my brother can hold his own on a ranch. Tess, my cousin, will be here to make sure everything runs smoothly.

The saddle I made for Tess is a beauty. The basket weave tooling looks smart and the leather glossy and dark. My enthusiasm for finishing it ramped up after Karen had stopped by the ranch.

Since Tess will never take any money for staying with Norburt, this gift is one way I can pay her back for her generosity and my peace of mind. I load it in the truck and take a drive over to her place.

Her husband, George, waves as I pull up. "Come in for a beer," he says.

"Sure thing." I drop the tailgate on the truck and haul the saddle out.

"Whatcha got there? That's a beauty." He runs his hand over the smooth seat and the basket weave skirt. "Is this one of yours?"

"Present for Tess. She helps me out, and no matter how much I twist her arm, she'll never take any money for staying with Norburt."

"Well, she shouldn't. Burt's her cousin too, and you know, she says it's a vacation to stay there. I'll be on frozen food, but I can handle that." George opens the screen door. In the kitchen, he pops the caps off a couple of Rainers.

Tess comes in from the back with a load of dry clothes in a basket. "I thought that was you, Miles. Is Norburt here…" She stops and looks at the saddle on the linoleum. "What's that?"

I laugh. "A token of my appreciation."

"Oh, Miles. It's lovely." She caresses the saddle, lifts it from the floor. "It's not that heavy, either."

I wonder she can see it because her eyes are swimming with tears.

I start talking to cover for her, give her time. "That saddle you've been riding must have come down to you through our grandparents. You can bronze it and mount your mailbox on it out on the highway."

We stand around laughing, and then she gives me a big hug. "I've got to try it on Thimble."

I hold the door for her as we walk out. "Should fit. I used a quarter horse tree with a short skirt." I smile. "Thank you, Tess."

I drive off watching her in the rearview mirror lugging that hunk of leather toward the barn.

I'm so glad she can be at the ranch because I need this time away. My whole life has become stagnated, sluggish and unwieldy. This adventure will freshen me up, spending time with a bunch of women from all over the country. Hell, maybe I'd make a regular thing of it if Karen wants to arrange this trip every year.

The day before I'm due to leave, Tess arrives with Thimble on her rig, and he's wearing the new saddle. "I thought Norburt and I could ride together, checking the cows. What do you think, Burt?"

Burt's grin says it all. He nods. "Yes, I'd like that. And Sis has put lots of good food in the freezer for us. Lasagna and pizza. Lots of fish and chips."

"Great. I'll have a cooking vacation."

❖

Early on the fifth of August, I back the truck up to the gooseneck trailer and drop the hitch. The morning is crisp, sun pushing up over Bull Mountain, throwing long shadows from the cottonwoods around the house. Cottontail bunnies scamper across the lawn, the dogs not yet on patrol.

I load all the supplies into the front half of the gooseneck horse trailer. Boxes of canned and dry food get checked off the list. I'd been to Van's in Helena for most of it, then the Real Food Store for the sprout seeds, organic peanut butter, and brown rice. Karen's list is complete and well thought out. Took me a whole day in town to gather everything.

Last to go on the rig is Buck. She has the whole rear half to herself, and I let her ride loose. I wing the truck door open, and Skipper jumps in, a flash of gray and white. Skipper rides beside me on the bench seat, leaning up against me, scooting closer every minute or so.

The drive takes me north of Helena through the Missouri River–carved canyon at Wolf Creek, then up the Dearborn River into big open ranch land. The secondary road to Augusta runs along the Rocky Mountain Front, that breathtaking place where prairie meets a rugged wall of peaks, craggy and wild with snow where rock meets sky.

I've always loved this little-traveled two-lane road with scattered ranches. At Augusta, I turn west toward the mountains. It looks like a solid wall blocking my way. As I near the massive front, they seem to open a rift at the side of Cyanide Mountain. It's a deceptively long drive to Benchmark.

❖

Charlene is definitely a cutie, I observe, as she climbs out of the truck. Blond hair down past her shoulders, pulled back in a ponytail, green eyes, body fit and tan, but oh so young. A little shorter than I am, I figure she must be five-seven, but way more curvaceous, filling her worn blue jeans in all the right places. Her green and rust plaid flannel shirt is buttoned up to a provocative height.

She looks me up and down with a half-smile. "You must be Miles."

"That's right." *One hot dyke if ever I've seen one.* "Long haul?"

"Not too bad. Six hours on the road. This your dog?"

"Yep. Skipper. She's a handy warning system for bear."

"That never hurts. Let's unload the stock and go over what we need to pack."

She's all business, drops the back ramp of the long gooseneck and starts unloading into the corrals. The horses and mules look good, seasoned and ready to go. Seven all together.

"That's a fine bay." I nod toward the butterfly among moths.

"My mare, Swift. Arabian and tougher than she looks." She winks with a small smile. "Like me."

I return the smile. "I can imagine."

There's another gal with her, Marty, and she helps get all the gear out: six Decker packsaddles, wall tents, and cases of cooking gear. I look at the growing pile and ask if she brought any hay pellets.

"Hay pellets? No. What do we need that for?"

"There's not a heck of a lot of grazing up there," I answer. "I brought ten bags in my rig, just in case. But we'll need to pack in more on the actual trip. I also brought ten bales of hay, three for tonight and some when we come out."

Charlene looks relieved. "Good you thought of that. We brought a few bales of hay we can feed in the morning. Let's sort the gear and see if we've got everything we need. Jess bought a dozen air mattresses, and here's the pump."

"Glad she took my suggestion. Those cots outfitters usually provide are guaranteed to give you a bad night's sleep."

I get my scales out of the truck and hang it by a rope from the gate crossbar, then bunch the gear into six piles. When we're satisfied each pack animal will carry an equal load, we cover them for the night with canvas sheets.

"Where will you spend the night?" Marty says.

"Right here. We can roll our sleeping bags out and be ready early." I glance up at the sky. "Supposed to be clear tonight. I brought some sandwiches in a cooler." When I say this, Charlene looks a little doubtful.

"The nearest café is in Augusta," I tell her, just in case she didn't notice all the empty miles.

"Good thing we stopped for lunch in Townsend."

"I'll get on back then," Marty says.

"Let Jess know we need another ten bags of feed pellets. Once we're set up in camp, we can run the stock out to graze for most of their feed."

"Will do. Don't have too much fun, girls."

We wave good-bye, then turn and look at each other. I think maybe we will.

CHAPTER FIVE

June 17—two months earlier

"Hal, those men from the DNR are here," Nancy said, coming in the front door.

Hal shoved his chair back from the kitchen table, the legs thunking on the linoleum, and then he rose to his full six foot height with a grace belying his three hundred pounds and burst out of the house. He stormed down the porch stairs toward the three men standing by the white SUV. A state shield on the side of the front door read Department of Natural Resources, Michigan.

"You! Get off my place." Hal marched up to the wavering group of men.

One of the men held out a warrant and said, "We're here to examine your farm for pigs that could be the source for some feral pigs doing a lot of damage to the environment. We have been informed that you raise wild pigs. We sent notice last week we'd be here."

"I don't have any. These pigs are all carefully bred crosses with Russian boar. I've been developing this cross for five years. They are all in fenced pens and none of them have gotten loose. There ain't no wild pigs here." Hal adjusted the shoulder strap on his overalls.

"The state of Michigan has issued an order that these pigs are an invasive species. Maybe you don't realize it, but we have three thousand wild pigs, which cause almost two billion dollars' worth of damage to the environment in our state alone. We can't risk your pigs adding to that problem."

"This is a farm raising domestic meat for human consumption. I don't run my pigs loose."

"We will allow you time to harvest your meat, but all the hybrids and Russian boars must go." The man held out the warrant.

Hal batted the paper to the ground. "I'm not killing my pigs."

"If you don't, we'll kill them and you won't get any compensation."

A different man spoke up. "We're here today to inventory your stock, not to kill them."

"Inventory? You mean figure out which ones and how many to kill." Hal snorted. "I heard that you DNRs went on the land of a man who raised them for hunting sport down in Texas and shot all his pigs."

"That's simply not—"

"Get off my land."

"That warrant says—"

"I don't care what it says." Hal turned around and lurched back to the house, reappearing shortly holding a shotgun. He stood on the porch, legs in a wide stance, his bushy eyebrows low, lower lip pushed out.

One man held up his hand, motioning for the others to get back in the SUV. "We can't do anything with this guy. Next time we'll come with the sheriff." They backed around and drove down the dusty driveway.

Nancy joined him on the porch. "You've done it now, you fool."

Hal spun around, his face red. "What am I supposed to do? Everything I've worked for all these years can be shot to hell. I've developed a market for these pigs, and nothing's going to stop me."

"What's going to happen now? We're up to our necks in debt." She began to cry, raising her apron to her face. "If you'd just stuck with regular hogs, none of this would have happened."

"Look, Nance, everybody raises those pigs. Don't you remember? We nearly lost our shirts trying to raise those domestic hogs. The cost of feed per pound was more than the price we got for the meat."

"Things would have turned around. Prices go up and down. You just wouldn't hold out. Wanted a quick fix." Nancy wiped her eyes with the apron. "Dad never would have let you take over this farm if you'd acted so irresponsibly. He turned all the land over to you plus a herd of purebred sows, and look what you've done with them—bred them to those nasty little foreign animals."

"Nancy. You never got it, did you? What we're doing here is different." Hal's voice softened. "Chefs love these hybrids. The meat is dark and tasty, you know that. We're the only ones offering the crossbreeds. That's why they singled us out." Hal took a deep ragged breath. "We'll be ruined."

"Then let's start butchering them. Sell the meat while we can."

"We'll flood our own market. No. They aren't going to force my hand like this."

"You are so stubborn. You'll have our backs against a wall. I won't have the children put through this."

"Put through what? Standing up for our rights?"

"Oh, Hal," Nancy said, jerking the screen door open.

Hal went to the barn to kneel on the hard ground. He raised his eyes up to the rafters and prayed. "Dear God, give me strength to stand up to these men from the government. To protect my family and the hogs you have left in my charge."

Dropping his head into his open palms, his greasy mouse-colored hair fell like a curtain. He scratched his beard, drew in a long breath, groaned it out, and then he lurched heavily to his feet.

❖

Two weeks later, July first, a registered letter arrived. The postman shook his head and hummed with sympathy as he handed it over to the addressee, Happy Porker Farm, Mr. Hal Biggs, along with a black government-issue ballpoint pen. Hal's hands shook as he signed the form and fumbled the envelope open. It told him he had until the twenty-fifth day of July to comply with an order to destroy his hybrid and purebred Russian stock.

"You all right, Mr. Biggs?"

Hal's expression was blank, his eyes slow to focus on the postman. "Everything's fine, Ted." He turned and marched to the house like a robot.

Nancy was shocked they would actually do this. "I'm calling the radio station. We've got to get word out that this is happening. Maybe they will want to come interview you."

"Why that's a good idea, Nance." He held his hands out to her. "Let us pray."

"I don't have time for that." Nancy turned back to folding laundry.

That afternoon a TV van drove up to the house. A pretty blonde got out, positioned a cameraman near the pigpens, and began filming. Hal came out to them, smiling, thinking a little publicity for his plight might be a good thing. Nancy had cut his hair that morning, and he had donned fresh overalls and a clean T-shirt. His wife had picked out a plain red one, not one of his beer slogan tees.

The reporter got him to stand with his back to the pigs and began the interview. When the camera wasn't on her, she held a lacy white handkerchief to her nose. "Mr. Biggs, could you tell us about your farm's breeding program and the recent difficulties you've had with the state of Michigan?"

Hal waxed long and lovingly about the farm and his piggies, pointing out their striped longhaired coats, friendly dispositions, and his safe, strong fences. He talked about the upscale restaurants that offered the pork from his farm on the menu. And he read from the letter he received notifying him that his crossbred and Russian pigs would be eliminated.

"What will you do when the authorities come to destroy your herd?"

Hal's smile froze. He stuttered, "They ca-ca-can't do that." His face reddened, a scowl crept across it. "Why don't they go shoot all the wild pigs? Like they killed the rabbits in Australia? It's plain wrong to pick on my pigs. Call them wild. Those tree huggers don't know a thing about farming. My pigs aren't hurting anything."

"But what will you do?" the reporter pressed.

In a small voice, Hal answered. "I don't know. My life is ruined. I turn to God in his higher wisdom to show me the way."

"Okay, cut. We're done here." As an afterthought, she turned back to Hal. "Thanks for your time, Mr. Biggs."

Hal stood in the barnyard watching the van drive away. Slowly he turned his head, watched his pigs lined up along the fence watching him. He lifted his eyes to gaze out over the farm. Soon all this might be gone for him. *Might have to take a job in town at the gas station or go to work for another farmer. Life with Nancy would be a living hell if that happened.*

CHAPTER SIX

July 24

Hal stuck the fencing pliers in his back pocket and turned to face the sound of a motorcycle roaring toward him. Hal waved to get the biker's attention. A skinhead in a black leather jacket with a red bandanna tied around his forehead skidded his bike to a sideways stop. The guy put one foot to the dirt, lifted his lip, and looked both Hal and his farm buildings up and down.

"Wow, man! So this is your farm! You used to talk about it all the time." The man snatched his bandanna off his head and wiped his face, stuffing it into his jacket pocket. He kicked his bike stand and approached Hal with his hand out, then grabbed him in a bear hug, pounding his back.

"What do you want?" Hal demanded.

"Hey, man. Don't you remember me? Mark from Kuwait? We were on that oil well duty. You were on patrol, and I was security."

"Yeah," Hal lied. He had no memory of this guy, but he did his best to forget that whole experience, anyway. "So, what have you been up to, Mark?"

"You've put on some pounds, man." Mark patted Hal on the gut. "Your wife must be a good cook."

"That she is. You should stay for dinner." Hal tried to place this guy into his desert past, but came up dry. He would have remembered those snake cold eyes above the toothy smile. "So, Mark, why are you here?"

"I stopped to visit with some other old army buddies and heard what was happening to you. I couldn't fucking believe it."

Hal took a step back. "Did you see me on the TV?"

"That was way cool, man. All the people who don't know what the government is up to will get an education with this one."

"Those bastards. Come on in the barn," Hal said, sending a glance toward Nancy, heading for the clothesline with a full basket of laundry.

Mark followed, unsnapping his black leather jacket.

"Here, sit down." Hal waved at a bag of corn mash. "Don't get much company." He laughed, trying for good buddy. "My wife's idea to get on the boob tube."

"She had a good one. You are a hero, standing up for what you believe in, protecting your home. Seemed to me you're getting the shaft."

Hal dug a bottle of whiskey out of a feedbag leaning against a stack of pig feed. "Have a snort?"

"Thanks. Dry trip."

"Where you from?"

"Texas. Just got out of jail." He wiped his lips on his camo sleeve.

"What were you doing in jail?" Hal took a swig, eyeing Mark carefully.

"Took liberties with a gal who nailed me for rape. Bitch. She wanted it, I could tell."

Hal raised his eyebrows.

Mark laughed. "Knocked her around a bit, too."

"So, how do you want to help me?"

"Any underdog of the government is a friend of mine." Mark took another long pull from the bottle.

Hal sat down heavily on a feedbag. He put his head in his hands. "They're going to ruin me. I'm over my head in debt, and this is going to push me into bankruptcy."

"We can keep them off your farm. A man's home is his castle, right? I'll help you defend it. They can't push you around, buddy."

"They're coming tomorrow."

"Here's what you need to do, brother. Send your wife and kids to stay with a relative. The two of us can stand up to them. The people are behind us, you have no idea how much, and they're talking about how wrong this is. They see you as a fine Christian man who's being pushed around by the guys in suits."

Hal looked up at Mark with hope in his eyes. He blinked a few times to focus on his new friend. "You came just in time." He stood, swaying. "We'll get those bastards."

"What kind of firepower do you have?"

"My shotgun here. A box of shells. I don't hunt or collect guns."

"Hold on to it. Those bastards want to take our guns out of our hands. With your gun and my handgun it's not much, but it will have to do. Let's eat, then move your truck around the back of the barn, in case we have to make a run for it."

"I'm not running," Hal said.

"Just in case. You don't know what those feds are capable of. I have some good buddies in British Columbia, in case we have to hole up."

That evening, after Hal sent his wife and kids to her sister's house just like a couple of bachelors, they drank beer and watched a survival episode, which took place on a desert island. Mark laughed at their antics, disparaged their efforts, "Just like a bunch of city kids. Don't know nothing about making it."

Hal found frozen lasagna and heated it in the microwave. When he removed it the center was still frozen, but they just ate around the hard part.

After a movie, a bad spoof of a thriller with Tom Cruise, which they took for serious, they turned in. Mark slept in one of the kids' rooms. Hal climbed into the queen-size bed, missing the slim comfort of his wife. He tried to remember just where he'd been stationed with Mark, but came up blank. *He must be okay though, right? Who would lie about that time? And it was nice not to be all alone defending the place. Maybe my prayers were answered.*

At dawn they were ready, if slightly hung over. Mark had insisted they pack the truck with survival gear, extra food, sleeping bags, and a pack. Mark positioned the truck behind the barn for a fast getaway. The men had a barricade of sorts in front of the barn. Mark ripped boards off the siding for gun slots. The sun climbed laboriously toward noon while they swatted flies and blotted the sweat from their foreheads with large bandannas.

"God, it smells. Don't you ever clean the pens?" Mark waved at flies landing on his legs, buzzing around his face.

"Why? They just crap them up again. I'm hungry. Maybe I'll go up to the house to fix a sandwich. Want anything?"

"I'll take a cold brewski."

Hal set his shotgun down and opened the barn door. What he saw made him slam the door again. "Two vans and a cop car are coming down the road. What'll I do?"

"Go out there and tell them to leave."

"Oh, yeah. Just like that."

Mark yanked the door open and shoved him outside. Hal

watched as the two vans escorted by a sheriff's SUV came to a halt and a bunch of men climbed out. The cop car parked to one side. "You Hal Biggs?" said one of the men.

"Get off my place," Hal said, waving his fist.

"We don't want any trouble," the guy in the uniform said. One man in full combat gear stood with feet spread apart, gun across his chest. A man from the second van got out and walked up to the fence holding the curious pigs.

A different man held up a paper, reading aloud, "You are hereby ordered to destroy your wild pigs. If you are unwilling or unable, we—"

"Damn right, I'm unwilling."

"Well, we have an order to do so. Go ahead, John." He nodded at the man with the rifle standing to one side.

The man shot the Russian boar. The pig squealed and fell. The rest of the pigs ran in a tight bunch to the far side of the pen. The man raised his rifle again.

"Stop!" Hal felt a hand on his arm and half turned. Mark straight-armed the shotgun toward him and then jumped back into the barn.

Hal took the stock and with two hands waved his gun. With a shock that blew him back against the door, the gun went off. Mark must have taken the safety off. One of the men staggered and fell. The others hunched down behind the vehicles.

Hal felt Mark grab his arm and yank him back into the barn.

Wood splinters exploded in a lethal rain on their heads. "Shit, the gun just went off," Hal said, staggering back.

Someone yelled, "Come out with your hands up!"

"Well, yeah. Let's get the fuck out of here," Mark said. They ran for the truck parked out of sight behind the barn, started it, and took off across the field for the far gate. Shots rang out as they crested a hill, shattering the side-view mirror.

Mark laughed. "Shit, man. You got him but good. Aren't you glad we packed the truck with survival gear last night?"

"Oh, God, man. I didn't want to kill anybody. What'll I do now?"

"We're doing it," Mark crowed.

Hal's head smacked the roof when the truck hit a ridge in the field. "Do you think I killed him? Maybe I just knocked him down."

"Hey, buddy. You're a hero. Of course you killed him, there was blood all around." Mark started singing, "Great big buckets of blood on the ground."

"Where'll we go? Do you have friends we can go to?"

"Yeah, I have a buddy over in Chippewa Falls, Wisconsin. where we can crash. How long will it take to get to Chicago?"

"We can't go that way. That's exactly where they will hunt for us. The best thing is to go over the Mackinac Bridge to the north. We could even go to Canada that way, meet up with your friends in BC."

"Okay. We'll go over the bridge, but not into Canada. They check your IDs. All the roads have checkpoints. This truck will be spotted, easy peasy. We could just walk across the border, but then we'd need to steal a car. No, for now we need to stay in the States." Mark made a right turn at the next crossroads. "We'll go north on the blue line highways. We'll ditch the truck after we get to my pal Jake's. Is there a map in here?"

Hal dug through the greasy papers in the glove compartment. "Yeah, here's one."

It had been folded and unfolded so many times, the seams were open slits.

Mark glanced at it and said, "Check out what we do after the bridge. We want to angle southwest."

"Looks like Highway 33 runs along the north part of Lake Michigan, then we cross a bridge into Wisconsin. I think Highway 64 runs west all the way to Chippewa Falls."

"Yahoo!" Mark pounded the steering wheel. "After Jake's, it is straight across to Montana."

"You got four bucks for the bridge toll?"

They drove all afternoon and through the night, the back roads slowing them down considerably.

CHAPTER SEVEN

July 26

Bridger opened the door of the hunting camp cabin to find two men on the front porch: one tall, wiry, slick-headed man in camo and one massive disheveled bearded fat man in overalls and a frayed T-shirt.

"What's up?" he said.

"We're looking for Jake. This his cabin, right?" the skinny guy said.

"Yeah. He's in town for supplies but will be back soon. I'm Bridger." He pulled a comb from his hip pocket and ran it through his shoulder-length blond hair. He snapped the rubber band back into place. Somewhat vain, Bridger would have been handsome except for his small eyes.

"I'm Mark, and this is Hal." Mark pushed past Bridger and sat down on the ratty couch. "Jeeze, it's hot. You got anything to drink?"

"Couple of beers?" Bridger said, raising his blond eyebrows and adjusting his ponytail.

"That'll do." Mark put his heels on the coffee table.

"Got anything to eat? I'm half-starved." Hal wandered into the kitchen.

Bridger eyed his girth. "S'pose so. How 'bout a sandwich? There's baloney and some chips."

"Boy howdy." Hal walked eager-eyed after Bridger, who threw a loaf of Wonder Bread and some baloney on the counter.

"Got any mayo?" Hal said.

"Hey, honey, make me one, too," Mark yelled from the living room.

Bridger wondered if these guys were queer.

While slathering on the mayo, Hal peered out the window. "Nice you live right by a lake. You fish for bass?"

"So damn many lakes in this state, it's hard not to live beside one. No, I don't fish, but I think Jake does. He's got a boat, anyway."

At the sound of a car engine, Bridger parted the curtains. "Jake's back."

Jake blasted through the door carrying a box loaded with food. "Who's truck is that...oh, it's you, Mark. What're you doing here?"

Mark took a lazy swig from his bottle of beer. "We're on the run, Jake. Hal, the guy in the other room, shot a fed."

"No kidding." Jake leaned back to see who he was talking about, set his box on the bench by the door. "Oh, shit. I heard about that. The pig thing, right? Well, you better ditch the truck. You guys are all over the news. Damn you for bringing it here."

"No problemo. Wondered if you can help us out with some grub. Maybe crash till the morning. We've been driving all night, headed west, and could use a leg up." Mark stood and said, "Hal. Come meet your host."

Hal came out of the kitchen stuffing the rest of the sandwich in his mouth. He stuck out one hand and muffled the words. "Nice of you to let us stay with you."

Jake ignored the hand, standing back to avoid the food

spray. "Look, I've already got Bridger to deal with. I don't need any gun-happy assholes."

Hal's face fell. "I didn't mean it. The gun just went off."

"That's even worse." Jake stared at Hal for a minute, and then turned to Mark. "You're going to have to leave. And take Bridger with you."

"But, Jake. I thought we were friends." Bridger earned an incredulous glare from Jake.

"Look, Jake," Mark said. "We don't need no dead-weight. We're heading into the mountains, crossing the Rocky Mountains and going north to Cranbrook. We have to cross into Canada by foot, and that stretch in Montana is the only way I figure we can do it without being spotted."

Hal's jaw dropped. "Walk across the mountains?"

Bridger's craggy face lit up, his small eyes aglow. "That sounds like a real adventure."

"What we don't need is an extra renegade to watch out for. Why are you here anyway?" Mark said to Bridger.

Bridger gazed at the rug. "Oh, it's a long story. I got fed up with my job and left."

"Big deal. Don't most of us?" Mark sat back down to eat the sandwich Hal had made.

"You planning to rough it in the mountains? I could use some of my survival skills, you know, getting around. Take me with you."

Hal said, "Yeah, Mark, we could use another hand."

"I've got an old beater that will get you there," Jake said. "Take it and ditch your truck. Get rid of it a hundred miles from here." Jake carried the box of food into the kitchen. "Leave in the morning. I'll pack some food for you."

"Gee, thanks, Jake," Hal said.

"Stay off the main highways. I tell you, they're looking for you, big-time."

❖

Hal and Mark woke up to the nutty aroma of coffee. They found Bridger decked out head to feet in buckskins, including moccasins, with a Bowie knife tied down to his thigh. With his trim beard and ponytail, he looked every inch a mountain man.

"Where did you find that outfit?" Hal said in admiration.

"Made it myself from deer hide."

"Stupid." Mark frowned. "Everywhere we go, you'll be remembered."

Bridger turned back to the stove and stirred the potatoes, ignoring Mark. "How many eggs?"

"I'll take three. You have any side meat?" Hal said.

"Hurry it up, guys," Jake said, coming in from outside. "I've put some food in the car. Here're the keys and directions to my buddy Karl's place in Jordan. That's north of Miles City, Montana. That'll put you half a day's drive from the Rocky Mountain Front. There are passes across the mountains, but you'll have to go on foot. Leave the car. Can't be traced to me, so we're all right there. Where did you say you're headed?"

"A bunch outside of Cranbrook, BC. Heavy-duty militia guys."

"You so sure they'll want you there?"

"Fuck, yes. This guy is a celebrity. Hal stands for everything they're fighting for."

Jake gave Hal a dubious look. "You got a map?"

"One that's falling apart."

Jake got a ratty one from a shelf. "You can take this with you. It's an old atlas, but the roads are still there." He put his finger on Eau Claire. "Stay on Route Twelve. Don't go on the interstates, except I guess you'll have to some around Minneapolis. You have cash for gas and such?"

"I've got a credit card." Hal spoke up.

The three other men gave him a deadly stare. "I can help out there," Bridger said.

❖

Staying on the back roads doubled the travel time, and even with switching drivers, they were exhausted by the time they reached Aberdeen, South Dakota, where they got a motel room. They ended up staying three days at Karl's place in Jordan. Karl had lots of beer and not enough company. Some of Karl's pals came over, acting like Hal was a celebrity. Slapped him on the back. "Hey, man. What you did was great, standing up to those bastards."

Hal glowed under the attention, a little part of his mind not so sure he was all that great. When they ran out of stories and had made up a few, they figured it was time to set out again. Midday, once again hung over, the three men left Jordan behind, driving into the glaring sun.

"Where's all the damned trees? This is all just flat as far as you can see. Bunch of stinking antelope and nothing!" Mark stared out the passenger window with his mouth hanging open.

Far off to the south, humped mountains looked like giant buffalo to Hal; soon they too were left behind. Bridger slanted the visor to keep the sun out of his eyes, sleep pulling him into a drowsing stupor. The right car tire hit the gravel along the shoulder for the second time, snapping him awake.

"You're done driving," Hal said. "Jesus, you are going to wreck the car."

"I don't think we're going to make it to the Rocky Mountains by the end of today. As far ahead as I can see, there's nothing," Bridger said, pulling the car into a field access road so Hal could take the wheel.

Mark checked his wrist watch. "Drive another hour, then we can stop in Great Falls at a motel. I'll drop you two off at a café, then check in. Meet up for a bite, then you and Hal can sneak in. That way the motel manager won't know what Hal and you, in your fuckin' skins, look like."

"I agree," Hal said. "It'll be better if we set off across the mountains first thing in the morning. I'm beat."

"We need to get an earlier start tomorrow."

Everything worked as planned. Meeting at the diner, they all ordered the meat loaf and mashed potatoes with green beans special. When it arrived, plunked down on the counter, Hal lowered his head. "Lord, I want to thank you for..."

Mark said in a hoarse whisper, "Cut it out. Just shut up!"

"You can thank me, because I'm paying," Bridger said with a sneer.

Hal frowned, picked up his fork, and said, "Don't you ever give the Lord thanks?"

"Just shut the fuck up and eat." Mark shoveled food into his mouth.

Later, they stood in the tiny dark brown motel room contemplating the one bed. Hal complained when Mark told him he had to sleep on the floor.

"One of us has to," Mark said. "Take a shower before we leave here tomorrow. The last hot water we'll see."

The next morning, a wall of mountains emerged out of the clouds, rising from the plain to block the way west. The rising sun tinted the snow pink. The men leaned forward, craning their necks to see the crests of the rocky massifs.

"Holy shit, man. We're supposed to walk across that?" Bridger rolled the window down and stuck his head all the way out to get a better view.

Hal was having serious doubts about this running from

the law thing. Maybe if he went back now, he could explain. Events had swept him up like a plastic bag in prairie wind, and he felt he had no control over where he went.

Nearly an hour's drive west of Augusta, the three men abandoned the car on a little-used ranch road and arranged the packs on the ground. Bridger laced up hiking boots, putting his moccasins in his pack. They sorted their food into three piles.

"Do you really think this is enough food to get us over the mountains?" Hal said.

"Look, you idiot, it's filling all our packs. Of course it's enough." Mark said, jamming food into the canvas backpack.

"Hey, man. Put the potato chips on top," Bridger said. "See, like this. Canned food on the bottom, then bread and lunchmeat, then the fucking chips."

"Mind your own fucking business," Mark said, tossing stuff in his pack, with one squinted eye on Bridger.

"Hey, could you guys clean up your mouths? I never heard such foul language."

Bridger and Mark instantly stopped what they were doing and stared at Hal. "You've got to be kidding," Mark said.

"No. I mean it. I didn't say anything about it before, but it has gotten to me. It's fuck this and fuck that all day long."

Mark turned his back on Hal and shouldered his pack. "I don't believe it," he muttered.

"Boy, this is some kind of country." Bridger gazed at the Rocky Mountains. His beady eyes were bright, and a smile filled with awe crossed his face. "Look, some of those mountains still have snow on them."

"Couldn't we have parked a little closer?" Hal fought off a rising whine in his voice. "Jesus, what have I gotten myself in for?" he said under his breath.

"Let's get a move on," Mark said. "It'll take us an hour or

two to get into the mountains. We want to make camp before dark. Here, Hal, you carry the duffel bag first. We'll take turns."

"Who's got the tent?" Hal said, hefting the duffel.

"We don't need no stinking tent," Bridger responded. "There's a tarp in there we can use if it rains. We're bivouacking, right?"

"What about bugs?" In response to Mark and Bridger's sneers, he defended himself. "You know, those little biting things that fly?"

"Jeeze, Hal, you've got to toughen up." Mark tossed Hal a can of Off. "Here, man. Use this."

"That's aerosol," Bridger said.

"So?" Mark screwed up his face.

"That stuff is bad for the environment."

Both Mark and Hal stared at Bridger. Hal held the can as though it might bite him.

"Global warming. Don't you know anything?"

"Fucking A." Mark turned to Hal. "We got a tree hugger on board."

"Oh, don't be so reactionary." Bridger shouldered his pack.

The men set off crossing rangeland, avoiding the roads. Scattered bunches of cows eyed them suspiciously from a distance. Four hours later, the mountains, backlit now by the setting sun, weren't much closer. They decided to camp near a stock tank marked by a windmill pump. The inside walls on the tank were green with strings of algae, but the water tasted good. In the morning, they filled their water bottles from it and set off in a foul mood.

Hal's stomach growled and blisters already were forming on his heels. Mark doled out the rations with a tight fist. Hal pulled out his overalls, noticing how roomy they had become.

"The food's not going to last long. Is there any place we can get some more?"

"You're eating more than your third, so stop whining." Mark passed out candy bars, handing the duffel to Bridger. "I don't see any stores around here."

In the afternoon, they crested a rise to discover a scattering of ranch buildings along a little creek. They dropped to the ground to eye the place through binoculars. After a few minutes, a woman came out of the house, got in the car, and drove out the long driveway toward the highway snaking black in the distance.

They got up as one, shed their packs, dumped the duffel out, then carried the empty bag down to the ranch house. Mark headed straight for the kitchen, diving into the cupboards, and Bridger took on the chest freezer. He said, "I could use some meat. Steaks or something."

Hal searched for the master bedroom. His quest was for thicker socks and some pants that fit, hoping the man of the house was close to his size. He was out of luck with the pants, a skinny size thirty-six long, but he found a nice Pendleton wool shirt. "Great. By the look of that snow…"

"Is that you, Nora?" a man's quavering voice called out.

Hal froze. He crept down the hall to find an old man in bed. They stared at each other in shock. Hal spun around and raced back to the kitchen. "Hey, you guys, there's an old man in a bed down the hall. Let's get out of here."

Bridger hefted the now crammed bag to his shoulder and they scrambled. Mark stopped at the gun cabinet and tried to open it, but it was locked.

"Come on!" Hal urged.

"Looking for some ammo." Mark pulled open the drawer under the cabinet and threw boxes of shells out, rising with two boxes and a big grin. "These will work in my pistol."

That night they ate steak and roasted potatoes feeling smart and like real wild men. The mountains were closer, and tomorrow looked good for getting on a trail into the wilderness.

Hal said, "I need to find some smaller pants. You guys are starving me to death. I must've lost twenty pounds since I left home." He thought of Nancy's cooking with longing. Peach cobbler, a nice pot roast or pulled pork enchiladas.

The next ranch they came to gave them a little more trouble. A woman was in the kitchen canning pickles when they came through the door. Mark held the gun on her while Hal asked her what size her husband wore.

She looked at them like they were crazy, stuttering out, "Why, he's a big man. Near like you."

Hal headed for the bedroom, rummaged through the closets, and came back wearing a pair of jeans only a little tight, the overalls draped across his shoulder. He carried three pairs of socks. Bridger took a wool sweater and some extra socks. He tossed Mark a red plaid wool jacket. "You might need this."

Bridger picked up an apple pie cooling on the counter. "My favorite." He smiled at the woman.

"My husband will be home soon, so you better clear out," she said with some courage.

"Fine. Come on, boys, it's a long way yet to Great Falls."

Their arms loaded with treasures, the men scrambled back to where they'd left their packs and quickly got on their way west. "Planting that idea of Great Falls was pretty clever, Mark. Now they'll be off our trail." Bridger wiped his mouth on his sleeve. "Steak two nights in a row. And pie. Say, boys, wasn't that good? This is livin' high."

Hal didn't agree. Burnt-in-the-fire potatoes and near-raw meat. The pie was okay, but not half as good as Nancy's. The crust was leathery instead of exploding into flakes with each bite. He longed for Nancy's lasagna, bubbling with sauce and cheese. And her applesauce cake with walnuts and cream cheese icing. He looked up to the wall of mountains iced with snow, and he shivered. Tonight would be another cold, hard camp. Dry, too. The whiskey had run out the first night, and the people must have been teetotalers at the last ranch.

Somehow, Hal had been sucked along on this trip like a piece of flotsam on the ocean. Floating trash, caught up with other unwanted or needed items.

CHAPTER EIGHT

"Hal. Get your butt off that rock and fix us something to eat."

"The hell with you, Bridger. What am I, your woman?" Hal finished unlacing the boot and, without removing his socks, stuck his feet in the cold, running stream. "My dogs are killing me."

Mark came out of the forest with an armload of branches and dumped it at their campsite. "So, are you losers going to piss around all night? Let's get a fire going and put some grub together."

"Hal's whining about his feet." Bridger spat on the ground, too close to Hal. He unlashed the Bowie knife strapped to his leg, and Hal gave him a quick look. "Let's cut that zucchini bread up. I could eat a horse about now."

Mark cleared a space for a fire, got one lit with the last of their candy wrappers. While they built up the fire, they chomped on the sweet bread. "Be dark soon. Where's that chicken?"

"Still frozen," Hal said, limping barefoot over to a duffel bag lying under a tree. He hefted it up and dumped it on the ground, then pawed through the pile. "There's a couple of cans of beef stew. A loaf of bread." He held the bread up and laughed. The bread was crushed inside its bag into an unrecognizable mass.

"That'll do for tonight." Bridger wiped his mouth on the sleeve of his buckskin shirt, fringes greasy and stiff.

Mark sorted through the pack with the pans and tin plates for the can opener when he heard a noise. He looked up. "What the fuck! Bridger why do you have to use that goddamn knife for everything? You've wrecked the cans."

Bridger just smiled as he sawed the lid off the can, huge jagged edges dripping with stew juice. He wiped his knife on the buckskin leggings of his thigh. "You want to use them again? Don't be such a sissy and bring the pan over here." He shook the cans out over the camp cook pot and set it precariously on the coals. The cans got tossed into the bushes.

"That's going to draw animals, you know." Mark laid out three plates and spoons.

"You ladies would never get anything done without me." Bridger leaned back against a tree.

Hal carefully arranged his socks on a stick by the fire. The once white socks were black with dirt and sweat.

Mark said, "You should rinse those out in the creek. No wonder your feet are killing you. Didn't you pick up some socks at the last place?"

"I'm saving them. Besides, mind your own business."

"It is my business if you can't walk tomorrow." He reached inside his Carhartt jacket and pulled out a map. "The way I figure it, we're just about here." He put one grimy finger on the map, but the others didn't look. "We can cross the border into Canada north of Polebridge. Pretty wild country up there."

"This isn't? How many days' walk to get over to the other side? I'm sick of these mountains." Hal stirred the stew, putting the spoon in his mouth to check the warmth.

"We crossed the Sun River about three hours ago and are now on the Indian Creek Trail, which goes up over the divide at White River Pass. Two days, I'd guess. Then we'll be down in the Flathead, at Condon. My buddy lives there, and he'll take us north through Polebridge. The border up there is like a sieve, you can walk through anyplace."

"Where in British Columbia are we supposed to meet up with that bunch?" Hal said.

"Cranbrook. Let's eat." Mark set three tin plates out on the ground.

Bridger hooked the pot with a branch and put it on the dirt. He spooned out his portion and sat back with a wad of white bread.

"You s'pose there's any feds after us?" Hal peered into the gathering dusk.

"Feds are after you, not us." Mark laughed. "You would have to shoot that DNR agent."

"What's the DNR?" Bridger said.

"Department of Natural Resources. You heard the story, didn't you? Shot my purebred Russian boar. Claimed there were three thousand wild pigs roaming the state, and my hybrids would get loose and join them. My fences were strong, and besides they loved me, would come when I called."

"So, they were on your pig farm. What were they worried about?"

"I don't know. Rooting around, I guess. A danger to the environment. Goddamn state of Michigan, deciding they can put me out of business by passing some stupid law."

"Oh, it was just a bunch of pigs." Bridger laughed.

"These were special. Chefs loved the meat, dark red, lots more flavor. They just came on my farm one day to shoot them. My life was ruined."

"What about your wife? And kids? Didn't you have kids?" Bridger said.

"She thought I was nuts. Well, she's got the kids to herself now. I'm going to get those bastards."

"You got one of them. There's some who'll join you, just on general principle." Mark stretched his legs out wide so he could scratch his crotch. "Those bastards stuck me in prison for five years. Claimed I raped a US Marshal. Well, I can tell you she liked it."

Bridger joined in. "Didn't you rough her up pretty bad? That's what I heard."

"She was mouthy."

Bridger gathered up the plates to wash off in the creek. He paused and said, "You served your time for that. What made you want to help us get to Canada?"

"None of your damned beeswax."

Bridger narrowed his eyes. "You did something else, didn't you? Come on. Tell us."

"Why should I tell you anything?" Mark jabbed the fire with a stick. "Search me why I ever offered to help you guys." He sprang to his feet, bristling. His fists were in a tight ball. "I should just leave you here on your own."

"Let's turn in," Hal said, attempting to head off the escalating confrontation.

The two men eyed each other from opposite sides of the fire.

"We have a right to know why you are on the run." Bridger stood his ground.

"I'll tell you when you tell us. You didn't just walk off your job." Mark spat on the ground.

"Okay. I filled up my briefcase on the way out."

Mark laughed. "Wasn't with reports, was it?"

"No. Now you."

Hal had thought this was all about him, now he was learning different. *I'm just a tool, a means to an end. God, how did I get into this mess?*

Mark rocked back on his heels. "After I got out of the pen, I hitchhiked north and stopped at a bar in Kansas. Stayed until closing. Waited outside for the bartender. She'd been flirting with me all night, but she put up a fight and I hit her a few times, choked her. Dead as a doornail. So I went through her pockets and found the keys to her motorcycle—the only thing left in the parking lot, and rode through the night. That's about it. Except I heard about you, Hal, and thought I could help you."

Hal frowned. "So, you killed that girl?" All three men sat silently for a moment. Hal seemed to shake himself like a bird dog leaving the water. "Gee, thanks for wanting to help me, but I have to say, I wish you hadn't."

"You'll thank me when we get to Canada. You'll be a hero."

"I never wanted to be a hero, just wanted to be left alone. Let's turn in."

❖

In the morning, they packed up and got on the trail at first light. They stopped midmorning for a break and to rummage in the food bag.

"How far is that so-called pass? We been walking all morning." Hal took a wad of white bread, flattened it between his filthy palms, then swiped some peanut butter out of the jar with his fingers and smeared it on the gray surface of the bread. "You said it was only a little way across these mountains."

"Looked like that to me. Soon as we strike a little creek,

should be Indian Creek, the trail goes off to the left, then gets a lot steeper up to the top," Mark said. "Hal, keep your fuckin' fingers out of the jar."

"Wasn't this one of the old Indian trails across the mountains?" Bridger said.

"How the fuck should I know. Am I an Indian?"

Bridger jumped to his feet. "What's that sound?"

"Somebody's coming! Let's get off the trail." Bridger grabbed a couple of bags and headed for the dense timber. Hal and Mark were right behind him, and they ducked behind some rocks and downed timber.

"It's a pack train. Only two riders. Let's jump them." Mark said. Bridger put his hand on his shoulder, pushing Mark down.

"Let 'em go. We don't need the hassle."

Mark said, "We could ride the horses. And we could use all that stuff those horses are packing."

Bridger said, "I don't know squat about horses."

"Me too. More trouble than they're worth." Hal ducked lower behind the rock.

A dog at the heels of the first horse moved to the side and stared in their direction. The dog's nose flared and it lifted one ear. After a sharp bark, the rider called to the dog, which turned and followed along.

"Are those women?" Mark said.

"No way women could do that," Bridger said, watching the lead rider on a chunky sandy-colored horse.

"That rider on the end has a ponytail."

"So?" Bridger squinted and pointed to his own.

The three men watched the pack train pass at a rapid walk.

CHAPTER NINE

"How did you find this place?" Charlene says when we ride onto the campsite. "This is a great spot."

"I'm lucky enough to know the outfitters who have the Forest Service permit." We tie the six pack animals spread out on the long log rail, then unload the panniers and pile the contents off to the side, sorting them into tents, food, and other gear. After we've unpacked the stock, we turn them all loose into the corrals.

The late afternoon has grown hot, and I'm working up a good sweat.

"We can place the packsaddles on the log tie-up and cover them with the canvas manties."

"Sure thing, boss." Her smile is patient.

A subtle way of telling me to butt out, she can handle it. My respect for Charlene grows. She's a hard worker and knows how to get the job done.

"Don't unsaddle your horse yet," I say. "The pack stock can go out on grass. If we're up early day after tomorrow, there'll be time to run them in before we leave for Benchmark. The trip out will be fast."

Charlene scans the ridges with a small frown on her face. "There's no way they can run off?"

"No. It's a blind valley. You lead, I'll drive. We'll be turning right once we cross the river."

We mount up and gather the horses into a tight herd and drive them out the gate.

At the river crossing, I call to Skip. "Here, up!"

I slide my leg back, and she jumps into the saddle, taking a boost on my stirrup. I hold her in front of me until the other side of the rushing water.

"Nice trick," Charlene yells out to me.

"Yeah. This river's a little strong for dogs."

Large rocks under the rushing water slow the horses to a careful crossing. The water is cold and crystal clear. Evening light slants through the trees, the horses and mules running through the light bars, flashes of sorrel, red bay, and black. They trot up the trail, hesitant to go to a strange place, but feeling good to be shed of the pack harness.

We don't take them deep into the valley, just stop at the first grassy meadow. They groan and grunt, rolling on their backs, hooves waving in the air, horseshoes flashing silver.

Back in camp, we attack the cook tent, sweeping the canvas floor and wiping down the table. I set a fire in the little stove in the corner against the chill of evening. We eat the last of the sandwiches and a can of peaches for dinner. After we've satisfied our hunger, we work for another hour or so setting up the kitchen, stocking the shelves.

I place a pad for Skip in the corner, and she doesn't need to be invited to curl up with her tail over her nose.

"I'm beat," I admit. "Let's finish this tomorrow."

"At least we can sleep under cover." Charlene lifts the tent flap to look out. "Might get some weather tonight." She lights a kerosene lamp against the growing dark. When she adjusts the wick, the rosy glow of the lamp warms her skin, making the freckles stand out.

"Was supposed to be clear. Predictions are about as useful as a bicycle is to a fish."

"What?" Charlene blows out the match, then looks at me like I'm crazy.

"Guess you're too young to remember that. It's an old feminist saying, 'A woman without a man is like a fish without a bicycle.'"

"Doesn't make sense." Charlene screws up her eyes, and then laughs.

"That's right."

Thunder booms, and we go out to watch the light show. Up the way we'd come, the lightning cracks like gunshots, and blue electricity sharpens the ridge of the mountains. Thunder rolls in waves, pushing the smell of ozone ahead. I feel something press my leg, reach down and ruffle Skipper's ears. "It's all right, girl."

Charlene raises her face to the approaching storm, her mouth open in a welcoming smile. The electricity in the air is contagious, the flashes of light making her face shine. She looks sideways at me, raising one eyebrow. "Storms turn me on."

I give her back a slow smile. "Are you going to be bad?"

"That's a matter of opinion."

"Truth is, I'm not a quick starter."

"Just put your arm around me and don't be so hard to get." She laughs and leans against me, so I do as she asks. "Isn't that better?" she says with a tiny edge of a grin.

So, we stand there, dog leaning against my leg, hot young, sexy dyke leaning against my side, her arm at my waist, watching the storm lighting the ridge tops, listening to the rain rip through the trees. I lower my nose close enough to catch the particular scent of her rising with her warmth. I find a place in me that was lost beyond reach, past my shriveled heart. The rumble of thunder throbs through my body. And yet, I feel a strange peace.

The rain approaches with the wind, pounding through the trees, sweeping toward us. Trees swirl, nearby we hear the crack of a breaking branch and its fall through the tree limbs.

When the rain mist touches us, we duck under the tent flap and let it fall back to the drum roar of rain pellets on canvas.

Once inside the tent, I'm shy. Spend some time settling Skipper, arranging my air mattress and bag near her, at least ten feet from Charlene's bag. She says something, but the rain is so loud I can't hear. "What?"

"You're a skittish sort," is what she said.

"What do you mean?" I am blushing like a newlywed teen.

"Don't you like sex? I mean, here we are…"

My mouth drops open at her forwardness. "I don't just jump into bed with the first—"

"Oh, come on! This is the twenty-first century. I'm not going to drive a moving van up to your ranch. It's just that you are very attractive to me, tall, strong, kinda butchy rancher gal."

"Look, it's not that you aren't about the hottest thing I've seen in ages, it's, well, I guess I'm an old-fashioned girl. I need a little time to get to know you."

She groans. "Okay. So let's hurry up."

My body tenses, and my eyes go shifty. "What do you mean?"

"I'll give you a little time, you know, to get to know me. I'm all turned on and no place to go. Storms do that to me."

"Oh?" I say, a little miffed. "You mean I didn't have anything to do with that? Any old port in a storm?"

"As it were." She narrows her eyes, and a lopsided grin spreads across her face.

"You have a new nickname, girl," I say. "Stormy."

"I like it. Now I want to hear something about your life. You know, the getting to know you part."

I relax a bit, lean back on my rolled-up jacket, and tell her about Jane. She had to draw near to hear over the roar of the falling rain. Stormy is a good listener, and it is easy to feel engaged with her about that hard time. I told her how I met Jane, how she came west, and how her life ended at Quail Mountain at the hands of a woman who hated her own queerness.

The rain lets up a little as I run down to a drowsy ending. I'm feeling very cozy and warm in the chill of the high mountain storm with Stormy murmuring soft responses along the story's thread. "I'm nodding off," I tell her, sliding deeper into my bag.

"Thanks," she says. "You're right, I feel closer knowing something about you. I've never lost someone I love, can't imagine how awful that is."

❖

In the morning, I awaken, with all meanings of the word, to a kiss. A kiss that skirts the edge of passion. Then she's gone back to her bedroll, gathering her clothes. Lying limp with one arm flung out, I feel Skip's cold nose on my arm, turn to see her intense stare from her one blue and one brown eye. "Dog, you are such a voyeur. But I guess you're hungry." She wiggles in agreement.

A sharp whinny from the corrals gets me up to start getting work done. I find my jeans, slip them on, and say, "You're up and functioning early, Stormy."

She laughs and says, "Oh? Is a kiss functional?"

I admire her as she runs her fingers through her tangled

blond hair and lifts her arms to her head, raising her small breasts, nipples erect. "Um, you could make today real difficult," I say.

Stormy winks at me and reaches for her flannel shirt. "That's the idea."

Can't help but smile at that. I go out and check to make sure the wind hasn't done any damage. Stormy joins me to dump a generous amount of pellets into the feeders for our two horses.

The three wall tents for the guests go up smoothly. I realize with longing, Stormy and I won't have much privacy once the trip starts. I glance over at her capable, long-fingered hands, and with no warning, my imagination takes them in a smooth glide across my breasts. I take in a long breath to cool the power of that vision.

I guess I'm pretty sure this is going to lead to intimacy. We can probably work it out.

Unpacking one pannier, I come across the sun showers. Black plastic solar shower bags filled with cold water can get comfortably warm in the sun. I fill two and set them out on the grass for later.

The sun heats up this morning like it had just returned from a vacation in the tropics. Trails of misty steam rise from where the sun hits the steep hillside across the valley.

By early afternoon, we are hot and sweaty, but done with the tents. We start on making the two outhouses decent. No one's put lime in them for a while, and they smell. There's a half bag in supplies, so I treat both the pits. Ashes from the small heating stove in the cook tent will have to do to keep the odor down during our stay. I make a mental note to try to pick up another bag of lime when we get back to Augusta.

As the day lengthens, I find I'm working more feverishly to finish. I want as much evening with Stormy as I can get. I glance over at her and realize she's doing the same thing. Our gaze connects with recognition, and she laughs out loud.

We work with urgent focus, knowing we won't have any time in the morning to luxuriate in our bedrolls. We'll be up at first light getting back on the trail. A certain electric intensity comes from the certainty that we will make love at some point. I want to and yet something holds me back. Is it loyalty to Jane?

The sun is sinking, taking the day's warmth with it. "Today went well," Stormy says. "We got everything done."

"And then some," I say with a half-smile.

Stormy pulls her shirttail out of her jeans, then wipes her forehead with it, giving me a flash of her waist above the band of denim. Her stomach is hard, skin shiny with sweat. She flaps the shirt a few times to draw cool air up over her breasts.

I swallow a gasp of desire. Warmth radiates over my thighs and belly. I shove cold air down into my lungs in an attempt to cool the embers. Quick and businesslike, I march over to the black bags lying on the grass. Lugging both the shower bags to the pole shower stall, I yell over to Stormy, "Come and get it! Oh, and bring a bar of soap and a couple of towels."

We peel off our clothes to hang them on bushes. I leave my shirt on and say, "You can go first."

She gives me a weird look. "Get in here and stop playing Miss Prude."

Holding one arm over my easy-to-hide breasts, I turn the spigot, sending out hot water over our sore and sweaty bodies. Stormy grabs the soap and we wrestle for the bar with sudsy hands, running our fingers into every crevice and over all the soft and muscled rounds, losing track of whose body we're touching. We're screaming and laughing like crazy women.

In the end, we are forced to wash our hair since it is already soaked. I hang the fresh bag for a good rinse.

Before we're done, we've checked each other for soap residue, slipping our tongues into those hard-to-reach places. Long after the water runs out, we revel in the slickness of our bodies. Desire has taken over my entire being, pulsing along my thighs and the lips at the opening of my body.

The kisses have ceased to be separate and now run into each other, beginning and ending. Our lips have become throbbing, sensing scouts of exploration.

I grab a towel to dry Stormy's back, then drape it over her shoulders. I get a second towel for my hair, the rest getting a once over. I reach for my clothes, scooping them into a bundle and heading for the tent. Stormy is right behind me.

We reach the sleeping bags, becoming still. My eyes are wide open, drinking in the woman standing before me, then our knees buckle and we go to the ground.

❖

Early in the morning, I get a little fire going in the stove to make coffee and fry up potatoes and onions. I brought a stash of half a dozen eggs in a plastic container in my saddlebags for a feast. While I'm cooking, Stormy goes to the corrals to dump feed out for our two horses.

She comes back through the tent flap with a big grin on her face. "I surprised a herd of a dozen mule deer enjoying the salt blocks in the corral. They held still, trying to make me think they were equine mules."

I smile, loving it that she is so tickled. "We'll have to bring another fifty-pound block of salt with us when we come back. Those stinkers will have it all cleaned up by that time."

She checks her watch. "Still early."

After breakfast, we celebrate by going back to bed. The return trip will be faster with the horses not packing any weight, and we use our stolen time wisely.

By seven o'clock, Skipper is helping us round up the pack stock. They haven't wandered far and are easy to drive back to camp.

CHAPTER TEN

The previous evening

Bridger looked up at the sky, boiling with black clouds. A silent flash of lightning cut through the skyline. The trail ahead was in the open, switchbacks climbing up to the top of White River Pass. The last trees were a small group of firs and some aspen off to the side of the trail. "Wait!" he called to Mark out in front. "We better find a place to shelter. A storm's coming."

Mark turned to glance at Bridger. "Don't be such a sissy. We can make it over the pass before dark."

"Not this boy," Bridger said. "That storm will be on us before we get halfway up. Come on, Hal. There's trees over there we can get under, set up the tarp."

Mark swore, kicked a rock so it bounced like a scared rabbit. He followed, muttering. "A goddamn bunch of lily-livered…"

Bridger found a sapling aspen under the trees and hacked it down with his knife. Hal shook out the tarp and cleared a space of rocks and dead branches beneath a large fir. Bridger tied the sapling across two low branches, lashing the tarp over the top, placing large rocks at the bottom. A serious crack of lightning made all three men jump. Long, booming rolls of thunder echoed across the bare mountain spine.

"Here, Hal. Tie the front corners of the tarp with this cord." Bridger left to search for some heavy rocks. When he returned, he placed them along the back edge of the tarp, securing the front to a couple of bushes. They pushed the packs under the flap and then crawled in for shelter at the next lightning bolt and roar of thunder. The air itself crackled.

Rain came down in sheets, sideways, swirling in under the shelter. They moved closer together away from the sides. Beyond the edge of the blue tarp, the rain formed a gray wall, pounding the ground, sending little torrents of water and fir needles past their feet, turning the dry duff to soup.

"Shit, man, I've never seen rain like this." Mark got on top of the duffel to get off the wet ground. They all sat on their packs. "Okay, I'll hand it to you, Bridger, we got this built in the nick of time."

"What do you mean 'we'? You were grousing the whole time about having to stop."

Crashing thunder drowned out Mark's reply. Wind moaned and whistled through the branches above their heads.

Hal looked up as though he could see through the tarp. "Lord, I hope this tree doesn't fall. Or some big branch."

The storm lasted into the night. Once the rain passed, the cold was numbing, wind cutting into the wet material of blue jeans, shoes, and socks. Any jackets that might have kept them warm were in the packs, wet. They huddled in a miserable, shivering lump until the cold sun seeped through their senses. Stiff and red-eyed, they stretched out their legs and arms, and then they crawled out from under the tarp and looked back at the mess of their belongings.

"We will have to build a fire and dry our stuff before we can go on," Bridger said.

"There's no dry wood here." Mark's teeth chattered.

"Over there." Hal pointed to a denser clump of trees. It was back the way they had come, and with reluctance they agreed that was their only prospect.

They picked all the soggy packs and gear out of the mud and half dragged the lot back to the stand of trees. They finally got a fire going with enough warmth to dry the clothes, scraped the mud off the packs, and sorted through all the gear. They roasted the chicken and, by evening, the men were in marginally better humor, well fed, and in mostly dry sleeping bags.

They were slow to start in the morning, but they crested the pass by the time the sun warmed, steam rising all around.

"Look at that," Mark said to Hal. "What did I tell you? Easy street from now on."

Bleakly, Bridger stared at the undulating expanse of mountains as far as the eye could see. Wind buffeted them, tugging at their jackets, threatening to lift their hats. It cut through the sun's warmth, whistling over rocks holding last winter's snow and through scraggly, shivering brush.

They scrambled down the switchbacks, aware of the cliff edge to their left. Bridger stopped to straighten his back and with a woof of surprise caught sight of the pack train coming back their way far below. "Hide," he called in a hoarse whisper. They desperately looked around for a hiding place on the rocky mountain trail, settling on some brushy growth a hundred yards to one side of the scree slope. A shelf of rock offered some cover.

"Get over, man, you're crowding me." Bridger jammed the gray canvas duffel bag down in front of them, hoping it would look like a rock.

The jingle of harness and clink of horseshoes grew louder. The horses were eager to get back to hay and grain and were stepping out at a good pace even on the steep incline. Before long, they were over the top of the pass, the sounds fading in the thin mountain air.

"That was close," Bridger sighed. "It's those same guys."

"Let's move." Mark led the way.

"Jesus, Mark. I thought you said it'd be a couple of days to get out of this godforsaken place. We've been hiking for five days and look at that!" Hal pointed to the west at folds of mountains fading into the distance. "There's nothing out there. We're almost out of food."

"Stop whining," Mark said, shouldering his pack. "It's smooth sailing now. I saw some elk as we came up the pass this morning. Maybe one of us will get lucky. It's your turn to take the duffel bag. And don't drag it this time."

"What would we do with a whole elk?" Bridger said. "We sure as shit can't carry an elk around."

"Dummy," Mark sneered. "We'll just take the best parts. Maybe you can make Hal a pair of elk hide moccasins, mountain man, and get him out of his crappy boots."

"That lightning had me nearly shitting in my boots. Hey, you guys, slow down!" Hal yelled.

It was late afternoon when they stumbled on the wall tent camp. Bridger looked around. "This is what those guys were doing. Setting this up. Well, boys, we have a dry place to sleep tonight."

They were like kids at Christmas when they discovered the cook tent and all the stacked food.

Bridger began opening cans. "Look around, guys. Find the canned meat. This shit is all vegetables and fruit." He speared a peach half and jammed it into his mouth.

Mark dumped the shelves on the ground and kicked through the cans. "Nothing. Not even one damn can of Spam."

"Beats nothing, which we had a lot of," Hal said. "There

are some potatoes. We can start a fire in that little stove and cook some up."

"Well, get with it. Least we won't freeze our butts off tonight." Mark took the bow saw from the tools stacked in the corner of the tent and walked off into the timber to collect more firewood.

A good topographic map was tacked to the front of the work counter. Bridger pried out the tacks, spread it out on the folding table near the light, and sat down to study it. "Mark's right, it's all downhill from here. If we follow the river going downstream, we'll come to the south fork of the Flathead River. Boy, if we could get our hands on a canoe, we could float all the way to Hungry Horse Reservoir. We'd bypass all that city stuff and come out above Whitefish. From there, it's clear all the way to Canada."

"By canoe?" Hal asked dryly. "And how're we supposed to get our hands on a canoe?"

"There's a bunch of ranger stations along the way. One of them will have one. If we ask him nice." Bridger leered. "Once we get to Whitefish, we can call that guy Mark knows, and he'll come get us. He could take us up near the border and let us off at a place we can cross."

Mark entered the tent with a large armload of wood. "Hey, let's get this show on the road. Am I supposed to do all the work?"

"We was just looking at the map," Hal said, busy cutting up potatoes. He shoved a stick of wood into the stove. "Bridger thinks we might get our hands on a canoe and float north to Whitefish."

Mark looked at Bridger. "That could work," he said slowly. He pushed Bridger out of the folding chair and examined the map. "There's a ranger station right here at the outflow of Big Salmon Lake where it meets the Flathead River. We can make that in a day of hiking, arriving under cover of dark. Slip the old canoe into the river and be on our way."

Bridger said, "Don't they take the paddles into the cabin? Kind of like the car keys?"

"If he did, then he's in trouble." Mark stood and began breaking up tree limbs. "We can stay here a couple of days, rest up a bit. Wash your socks out, Hal."

CHAPTER ELEVEN

S tormy and I spend most of the ninth of August in our hotel room. Resting, we call it.

Stormy untangles herself from me and says, "The only thing wrong with yesterday was the six pack animals between us." She stretches out and puts her feet on the floor, turns and looks at me. "You are some kind of woman, Miles."

"Wonderful thing, lust. You weren't anything I ever dreamed up happening on this excursion."

"Life is full of surprises."

"We'll make the most of it, eh?"

She just smiles. "I'm dying for some coffee. How about you?"

"Are you bringing it back? Or do I have to get dressed?"

"I wouldn't think of making you put clothes on. Black?"

I nod and settle back on the lumpy mattress, draw the sheet and blanket up to my chin. An afterglow of sex infuses my body, humming with pleasure.

I can smell the coffee before she opens the door. The tab on the lid gets in the way, so I peel off the plastic lid and take an unrestricted sip. "Mmm, good."

Stormy stuffs pillows against the bed's footboard.

"Long way away," I observe over my cup rim.

She leans back and says, "I like to look at you."

I huff. "Not a vision of loveliness this morning, I expect. What've we got, a couple of hours before Jess is due at Benchmark?"

"That's about right," Stormy agrees.

"So, tell me something about yourself. I know nothing, well, not much."

"I was born in Japan."

I sat up more. "True? You're not putting me on?"

She shook her head. "My parents were in the diplomatic corps. I was four when we moved to the States. Washington DC, to be exact, where I grew up."

"I took you for a ranch girl."

"From my earliest memories, we came every summer to a dude ranch in Wyoming. Dad stayed two weeks, then went back to the city. Mom and my brother, George, spent the month of August there. George was puny, always sick, so Mom thought it would be good for him. He hated it. I discovered my element.

"The wranglers were really nice to us kids, and before long I was helping with the horses. When I was fourteen, I talked my parents into letting me come and work there for the whole summer.

"They thought I'd last a couple of weeks of real work, but I loved it. Up at five, gather the riding stock, grooming, saddling, and riding out with the guests. Recently, I've started thinking about going to veterinary school. I sent an application to University of Washington."

"You are one of those people who were dropped off by the stork at the wrong address."

Stormy tosses her head back and laughs. "My parents think so."

"Okay. So I'm wondering how you figured out you love women. Not the easiest thing to do in the wilds of Wyoming. I speak from experience."

"I'll bet you do. The summer I was nineteen, I'd graduated from high school and was taking a break before college. Another wrangler came to work at that dude ranch. It was electric from the start. Got us both fired. Funny, all those years of the owners being so nice was right out the window when it came out I was gay. We lived in Bozeman for a while, but we were only part of who we were without horses, and the electricity got a short in it. Then I met Jess and went to work for her."

"Is she a lesbian?"

"No. I'd say she's asexual. Maybe she was once, but I don't get a glimmer."

"How long have you been working for her?"

"Couple of years."

"That makes you, what? Twenty-three? Still shitting yellow."

"Twenty-three is correct. What are you, ready for Social Security?"

"Not long. Forty-one."

She places her coffee on the nightstand and nuzzles against me. "An 'older woman.' "

An hour later, we drive to Benchmark to care for the stock and wait for Jess to arrive with the riding horses. I'm curious to meet this woman.

Skipper is happy to see me, wiggling out from her bed beneath the horse trailer. I give her some steak trimmings from last night along with her dry food.

Stormy and I practice keeping our hands off each other. Works pretty well. She's a devil.

Around three in the afternoon, Jess pulls up looking frazzled. She's medium height, thin in an underfed sort of way. Her brown hair is cut with not an ounce of style. We do one of those perfunctory handshakes, and then get to work settling in the stock. She starts right out barking orders to Charlene about unloading the horses, but seems wary of me, not yet fitting me into place.

Jess nods over toward a light blue two-horse trailer parked off to the side. A temporary pole corral circles the end of the trailer and takes in an area of the small creek that waters the larger corrals. A handsome white horse is watching us. Jess says, "What's that horse doing here?"

"Belongs to one of the guests."

Jess turns in disbelief to stare at me. "Who allowed that?"

"I understand your concern," I continued in spite of Jess's sputtering. "But this horse is a distance competitor, and is over being precious around other horses and on the trail. The care of the horse is the responsibility of the owner."

Jess gave the lovely Arabian mare one more long and disapproving glare, snorted, and went back to her chores.

Eighteen head cram into the two large corrals, sorted into one group for riding, the other pack. We toss piles of sweet alfalfa hay, one horse space apart all around the perimeter. Jess has roped four more bales to the top of her rig. She says, "We'll feed out those in the morning. Let's shift these bales into the back of the trailer. I can lock that. People will steal anything that's not locked up."

Stormy rakes manure out of the back of the rig while Jess and I unload the truck.

One more sweep of the area, and we're satisfied all is ready for tomorrow. I tousle Skipper's ruff, tell her what a good dog she is, and leave her with a bowl of dry food. She can get fresh water from a small creek that runs through the edge of the corrals. "Wish you could stay with me in the hotel," I tell her. She wags her tail across the dirt in long sweeps. "I'll be back, bright and early."

"What did you bring your damned dog for?" Jess strides up to me. "I don't allow people to bring pets."

"Skipper's not a pet." I stand and face her off.

"What use is he? You'll have to leave him here with someone." Jess's scowl is sour. She must be trying to piss me off.

"Skipper is a she and is coming with me."

Jess humphs, turns on her heel muttering about "...all these goddamn pets," and makes for the truck. She locks it down like Fort Knox and stands with her hands on her hips.

If I do this again next year for Karen, I'll urge her to find a more congenial outfitter.

It's a silent ride to town in my truck with Stormy trying to keep her face under control, sitting between Jess and me. While Jess is looking at the scenery out the side window, Stormy gives me a half-smile and a quick wink.

When we return to the hotel, we find all the guests have arrived and are in their rooms. We barely have time to shower and put on clean clothes to get presentable to greet everyone and go out for dinner.

Karen flew to Great Falls this morning, rented a van, and gathered all the women and their luggage. She arrived while we were caring for the stock and picking up Jess. We feel like old friends as we greet each other.

"We're all set," I say.

"Great to be here. You underplayed the scenery," she says, her brown eyes so warm and expressive.

"Kind of hard to describe. Good to see you again."

"Likewise, I'm sure," she says with a playful grin. "All the women are in their rooms settling in. Any good ideas about where to go for dinner?"

"There's a café across the street," Jess says.

"Pretty slim pickings, especially for vegetarians. How about a drive to Choteau to the Red Log Cabin? I know that's a fine restaurant, and we'll want a good meal under our belts for tomorrow."

"How far is that?" Jess asks with skepticism.

"Thirty miles, but well worth it for the pie alone."

"Has my vote," Karen says. "Miles, can you call and warn them there'll be twelve for dinner? I'll go round up everyone."

We all pack into the van Karen has rented for transporting everyone, Stormy, of course, squeezed in next to me.

On my other side is a gal named Candace, pressed in a little closer than necessary. Plastic cat barrettes hold back the sides of her mouse brown hair streaked with blue, which can't be more than earlobe length. Her main earrings are large copper disks, with assorted studs in any available earlobe space. She chats me up about her drill team riding in Maryland, letting me know she is an experienced horsewoman. "Honestly, we had so much fun. Then, like, I got unstraight, and it wasn't so much fun, you know what I mean."

Candace is wearing what she wore on the airplane, leggings with a hole in one knee, which I suspect was self-inflicted, and a tiny purple undershirt covered by a see-through lace shirt.

Everyone is high, joking. The women are decked out in their new jeans and flannel shirts for the ride to Choteau. The standout wears a light cotton long-sleeved shirt under an Ariat windbreaker and well-broken-in blue jeans. I'm pretty sure she's Rachel, the distance rider and owner of the white mare. We've spoken on the phone about the horse, and now I catch glimpses of her distinctive profile as she actually engages Jess in a conversation, which Jess appears to enjoy.

We help a waitress push tables together and gather enough chairs. The four trip leaders spread out around the table. Stormy is across and to the right of me, Karen and Jess at the other end of the table. The lean woman in the Ariat jacket pulls out the chair beside me, sticks out her hand, and says, "Hi, I'm Rachel."

"Right. Miles. One of your trip leaders," I say with a grin. "We talked about your mare on the phone."

"I remember," she says with light in her eyes. We exchange one of those mutual, assessing smiles, eyes busy. Rachel's no-nonsense but stylishly cut brown hair frames a tanned face with squint lines at the outside corners of her warm, chestnut brown eyes, formed by the hundred-mile gaze and good humor.

I pull out my chair and continue sorting the different faces, the personalities: eight women, all distinct individuals with a drive to do something they've always dreamed about. The excitement is high and they besiege me with questions once we are introduced.

"Is it really twenty-four miles?" says a gorgeous woman, enhanced by makeup and jewelry with gray-blue eyes and chestnut hair. She's flirting with me. "Luci is the name." She reaches across the table and offers her ethereal hand. Our fingertips touch, and it is oddly erotic.

"Every mile will take your breath away. It's rugged country." I smile at her, releasing her feather grip, thinking she near stops my breathing.

"It took me a week to whittle down what I want to bring to thirty pounds. Is that really *all* I'm allowed?" Luci laughs.

"Yes." I smile. "Guess you'll have to leave your hair dryer and makeup bag behind."

To her credit, she laughs uproariously along with everyone else. "Anyone else here from California?" she says.

"Michaela and I were married in San Francisco. I'm Sue." The Asian woman lightly touches her partner's arm, a hulking, six-foot redhead who gives everyone a half-smile.

Michaela says ,"Call me Mike."

"I used to live in California," Roseanne says, "but I went back home to North Carolina to take care of my mother."

Here's one to watch, I think. Not really the athletic sort.

Candace raises one eyebrow at Roseanne. "Like, is there much queer action in North Carolina?"

Roseanne stares at Candace for a moment, and then makes a pursed lip humming sound. You can see her make the decision to not answer, and she looks over to me. "My mother grew up in Great Falls, and she always wanted to travel to the Chinese Wall." In a hushed voice, she added, "I have her ashes with me."

"Oh." I clear my throat. "Do you plan on scattering them up there?"

"Yes!" she says brightly, then worry crosses her face. "There isn't a law against doing that is there? I mean, since it is a wilderness area?"

"Hell, no. Just the bears and us will know."

"What about bears?" Roseanne's voice quavers. "I am just utterly terrified by them."

Luci pulls her vest open to display her T-shirt with vivid red print across her breasts. "Score, Bears 8, Tourists 0. I got this in Glacier Park last year. Great, eh?"

"Bite me!" says Candace.

Tentative laughter comes from Roseanne, but nearly everyone else guffaws. I love Luci's brazenness.

I try to defuse the bear fear. "Sure, there's grizzlies in the Bob, and we might see one, but they tend to stay away from large groups. The Great Bear Wilderness Area is to the north of the Bob. We might hear the howl of a wolf but are unlikely to see one. We will see elk, whitetail and mule deer."

"What's the fishing like? I brought my fly rod, and I hear the trout are waiting for me." Rachel sets her menu down and slides her reading glasses low on her nose to look at me. I like her right off.

"You'll be kept busy, Rachel. I brought my rod, too. You'll see some huge bull trout, but they're all catch and release. Lots of rainbow and cutthroat, though. Maybe we can all have fish one night."

Kamau, a young, muscular African American woman whose close-cropped tight, curly hair could help her pass for a boy, says, "I don't eat meat. There's not going to be meat on this trip, is there? I understood…"

Karen says quietly, "All the food is vegetarian—partly in principle and partly because, according to Miles, the smell of meat draws animals to camp. I've found one can have delicious meals without it." She nods to the fisherwomen. "Of course, Rachel and Miles are welcome to share the catch with anyone who eats fish."

I'm starting to put the women's faces to the applications I read back in May. A couple of them, Roseanne and Barbara, had never ridden horses until they took the lessons for the trip, but I'm not worried about Barbara. Her hobby is running marathons. Kamau and Sue had done the lesson and show thing as children, and Rachel, Mike, Luci, and Candace are all horsewomen. Mike is a western cutting buff, Luci rides English on trails in Grass Valley, recently finishing some shorter distance competitive rides, Candace exhibited in drill teams until last fall and has since then taken up dressage. And I wanted to find out more about Rachel. I knew she competed in one-hundred-mile distance rides on the white mare, Kestrel.

Roseanne might be trouble. Somehow I doubted her diligence in preparing for the trip. Barbara was coordinated and fit enough to handle any sport. I imagined Candace might be in for a lot more than she figured on, perhaps complacent about her riding background. Well, we'd find out about the others soon enough.

"Make sure you bring your bags to Jess by eight this evening so we can take them with us in the morning to put on the pack animals." I look at Jess for confirmation, but she's talking to the woman next to her. "There are saddlebags on each horse for things like cameras, a jacket, and toiletries. You have the rundown on Karen's trip guide. In the morning, she will hand out lunches, but remember to fill your water bottles tonight."

"And leave your hair dryers with your extra luggage in the hotel storage," Stormy pipes up. "We don't have an extension cord long enough to use them in camp." She grins over at me, and I realize I've been neglecting her. I'll try to make up for that later.

By the time the entree is served, I've pretty much got a handle on everyone. I decide that during dessert I can change seats to the far end of the table to engage with the athletic gray-haired woman, Barbara, and Sue, who is on the other side of her hulking spouse, Mike. It's a good bunch, and Karen is charming as she engages each woman. Jess, on the other hand, is quiet and almost seems jealous of the attention I'm getting.

Candace is paying me a bit more attention than I want, however. Across the table from me, she is pretty ramped up, flirting like crazy. Stormy has a half-smile on her face, watching the show. She arches one eyebrow my way. A surge of desire sweeps me, recent and anticipated sexual images merging into warmth that floods my entire body.

With great effort, I disentangle my desire from Stormy

to make the supreme attempt to refocus on this somewhat annoying girl across from me. I've already heard more than I want to about Candace's seventeen-hand thoroughbred, his marvelous frame and movement, and the high-level awards the two of them have won.

The dinner is good. I devour a thick, rare steak, my last for a while, the buffalo chips, and a lush green salad with blue cheese dressing. I get some frowns from the confirmed vegetarians, but nothing too judgmental. Stormy has braised chicken and most of the other women get the Grecian shrimp on linguine. Rachel also got the steak.

"Save room for pie," I comment, ordering a slab of the Log Cabin's famous peanut butter cream pie. Most women watch their waistlines so close they don't even think about dessert. "You'll wear off the calories tomorrow."

"Is the apple good?"

"Personally, Rachel, I like all their pies. Most of the time, they have at least twenty different kinds. Branch out. Try something new." I say to the table in general, "Huckleberry is a Montana treat."

"Isn't that a lot like blueberry?" Kamau says.

"Yes, but the berries are smaller with more flavor," Rachel says. "I'm getting that."

After we've ordered dessert, I say to Karen, "Let's switch seats. I'll be on the pack string all day tomorrow, and this is my only chance to get to know everyone."

She gives me a big grin, and soon I'm sitting between Roseanne and Barbara. Jess has switched with Rachel, who is now opposite me, next to Sue. As I face Rachel to ask her about herself, I think how alike we are. We could easily be sisters. Not that we look alike, but we both grew up with horses in wide open country with the scent of sagebrush and nothing but mountains to frame our horizons.

As an opener, I say, "You have a ranch north of the Big Belts?"

"It's more on the east slope, not far from Lewistown. Closest town is Buffalo, which isn't really a town. If you expect to buy anything there except a pop or a stamp for your post card, you'd be disappointed."

"Cattle?"

"No, I raise endurance horses. Oh, I have a few cows to teach the horses to chase them and do basic ranch work. I brought my best mare with me, Kestrel." Rachel gave a slight indication toward Jess with her full lips. "I got a lecture during the van ride to dinner. Laid out all of what I could and couldn't do."

"Jess likes to be clear." This brought a snort from Rachel. "I saw Kestrel. Nice horse. I brought my mare, too. And my dog, and I'm not so sure that struggle is done."

"Would you mind tossing my horse a couple of sections of hay out of my trailer when you get there? By the time I arrive in the morning, she won't have time to eat."

"No problem." We study each other's faces. From the outside of each eye, a fan of wrinkles marches across her cheeks and into her ears. Her warm and lively brown eyes are brindled with green.

"So, why are you on this trip? You could do this ride without any support. In and out in one day, with extra time to take in the view."

Rachel picked up her dessert fork, studying it carefully. "Guess I'd have to say I was longing for the company of lesbians. Where I live, they're as scarce as postage stamps in Buffalo." She took a deep breath, the kind that goes all the way to your toenails. "The woman in my life, name of Margaret, pulled up stakes last fall. She didn't want to go through another winter. Went back to Boston."

I nod in understanding, as we hold each other's gaze. "Been there. Can get pretty isolated on a ranch."

Luci jumps in to the conversation. "I have a ranch in California."

"How many acres do you have?" Rosanne says.

"Twenty. So, how many acres do you have, Miles?" Luci raises her eyebrows at me.

I look at my spoon. Shift a little bit. Clear my throat, but say nothing.

"Well, come on. It's not a secret, is it? You must have tons. A hundred and fifty acres? A thousand?" She says like it is the most absurd number she can come up with.

I look at Rachel, and once she speaks, I realize I was appealing to her to do just that.

"By Western custom, no one says how much land they have. It's just one of those things that isn't done. You're considered a bragger if you have a lot, and a failure if you don't. It is also considered the utmost in rudeness to ask. And if you did say, it would never be in acres. Land is figured in sections or square miles, so you'd say something like, 'I'm running forty pair on the Lone Pine sections.' And, in fact, many ranchers don't know how many acres they have."

Luci's mouth drops open. "Square miles! More than one? You have got to be kidding!"

I squirm in my chair with a twist of a smile on my lips. I glance over at Rachel, who has a more open amused smile on her lips. I nod at her in thanks, and she gives me a nod back.

I say to Luci, "The land won't tolerate overgrazing. You figure the grazing density at one head for every twenty acres, which is forty head to a section. After a month, you move them to a fresh section or graze half the number." I watch Luci's face as she calculates land growing grass and livestock mouths.

By the time we pull up at the hotel in Augusta, I'm almost

as excited as everyone else for this trip to begin. Much to my disappointment, we decide Jess should ride with us to the corrals in the morning. I'm almost willing to deal with all the livestock just to be alone with Stormy. Karen will arrive in the van with the guests at six thirty. Gives us about an hour of dawn daylight to get everything done.

Stormy and I hit the sack early, small wonder as we were planning on getting out ahead of the others to prepare for the onslaught at Benchmark. We try like the dickens to keep our noise level down in this old hotel with thin walls.

In the morning, I pick up three large coffees from the café across the street, opened early just for us. "Sorry," the owner says. "The grill's not hot yet, or I'd fix you something to eat."

"That's okay, we've got some granola bars." I smile at her.

We're finishing tacking up the last two horses as Karen parks the van near the corrals. I have to laugh watching the women crawl out of the van barely awake enough to function.

"My God! Are we really crossing those mountains?" Barbara is mesmerized by the view.

I say, "We follow the Sun River Valley for a while."

Rachel vaults out. "Where's my rod? Is it safely stowed?"

"On that roan mule, wrapped inside sleeping bags."

"Oh good!" She is about to leap out of her skin, she is so exhilarated.

"I gave your mare two flakes of hay."

"Great." She goes over to the stall size pole corral. Kestrel nickers to her as she approaches.

"Which is my horse?" says Luci, the lipstick lesbian.

"We're giving you the black mule. Name's Jolly." Jess points out the rather sullen long ear with one eye rolled back at us.

"A mule? I thought I'd have a horse." The woman looks at the mule with pursed lips. "They're like, pack animals."

"You'll be surprised at how smooth and sure footed they are," I soothe. "Lots of riders prefer them. Call them the Cadillacs of the equine world."

Jess gives me a look.

Luci approaches the mule with her fingertips out. The mule ignores her, so she wisely scratches him behind the ears. "Kind of cute."

Kamau, the androgynous black woman, approaches Luci, leading her palomino mare. "This," she says, waving her hand in a presentation sort of way, "is Trigger. Won't you be jealous when I'm on top of her?"

Luci turns to her, virtual antennae on alert. "I could be when you put your strong legs around her."

"Yes. I plan to do that. And you? Do you ride astride?"

I smile and duck out.

Karen hands each of us early risers a cheese and egg sandwich and a bottle of orange juice. "Thanks," I say. "Was sure I'd be chowing down on granola bars."

Jess announces to the group, "Each horse has saddlebags for your lunch and any personal gear you want close to hand today. Hope you all brought your cameras. I hear the scenery is spectacular."

Karen passes out bean and cheese burritos wrapped in foil, a bag of trail mix, and an apple for each rider to put in her saddlebags. "We'll take a short lunch break halfway."

Jess knows her horses, and she's busy pairing up the riders with suitable mounts. The women climb on looking like eager spaniels. Most of them sit primly like Eastern riders. I know this will wear off by the end of the day.

"Oh, dear," says Barbara, the runner from Seattle. "This

saddle has so much leather." She laughs. "The saddle I rode in lessons was way smaller."

I just know Jess is about to launch into a disdainful lesson on Western saddles and their superiority, when Karen pipes up with, "I know what you mean. Those English saddles are so tiny, aren't they?"

"You'll be glad of them by the end of the day," Jess mutters.

I have to agree with her, but she's so superior.

Everyone is mounted up on her selected steed, and I nod across to Jess for a conference.

"If you stop for a short break at the suspension bridge over the Sun River, Charlene and I'll catch up with the pack string there, pass and lead on. There are no turns to foul you up, just stay on the road through the campground and follow the trail."

"Right." Jess steps forward and raises her voice. "Now here is something you all must know," says Jess with another of her announcements. "No one is to dismount on the trail without one of the wranglers standing beside your horse. Or mule, as it were." She glances at Luci. "This is a safety issue. You can walk alongside your horse in some places if you want a change from riding, but wait for someone to assist you."

Jess heads out, checking over her shoulder often. Roseanne is immediately behind her, with the most horse-savvy woman, Rachel, just ahead of Karen.

Before Stormy and I can leave, it takes about half an hour to get the rest of the Decker packsaddles on the stock, loaded panniers fixed in place and diamond hitches tossed across the canvas manty-covered loads.

The pack string is all ready to go, and I say to Stormy, "Let's line them out." I mount Buck, slap my thigh, and Skip is right there ready for another trek over the mountains.

CHAPTER TWELVE

L et's stay one more day, Mark. There's no rush, and I sure like those air mattresses."

"I'll second that," Bridger said. "I'm not at all anxious to cross that river to follow the trail. Did you get an eyeful of those rocks in the river? Big like bowling balls. By the map, there are two crossings we'll have to make."

"I'm tired of vegetables. Never much liked them." Hal curled his lip.

"If you girls want to turn this into a resort, I have to have some meat," Mark said.

"There's some deer out by the salt lick," Bridger said, his eyes bright.

Mark pushed out the tent flap, and then crept to the side of the corrals. The three deer bunched together, only mildly alarmed, accustomed to being safe in this place. He cocked his pistol and shot a young buck. Two of the deer bounded over the fence and crashed through the brush. One deer fell with a bleating cry and struggled to rise.

Mark approached within three feet and shot it twice more.

Bridger and Hal appeared at his side with eager faces.

"Hey, that was fast!" Hal walked over to the dead deer. "Now what do we do?"

"Eat," Mark crowed. "Let's hang it from that tree. Get some rope, Hal. There's some in the corner of the tent. Bridger, you're the one with a knife. Gut it."

Bridger and Mark grabbed the deer by the antlers and dragged it over to the tree. Hal showed up with the rope, uncoiled it, and threw the end toward the branch. After three tries, he swore and threw the rope in the dirt.

"Here," Bridger said. "Tie something heavy to the end."

All three men looked around. Mark picked up a rock, wrapped the rope around and tied it tight. He threw the rock up and over the branch. Trouble was, the rope dropped back down.

"Get something from the tent," he ordered. "Like a hammer, or that cast iron skillet."

Hal came back from the tent with the skillet. He tied the rope to the hole in the handle, and they got the rope across the branch, but it was too short and followed the skillet. They had to do it a second time, keeping hold of the end.

Mark tied the rope to the deer's antlers, and they pulled it off the ground.

Once they got the deer hung, Bridger set to work on the carcass, slashing into the belly. The guts fell out on the ground, blood poured out of the cavity. He stood back, looked at his bloody moccasins, then waved his toe toward the mass of intestines. "Get that out of the way."

Hal took a stick and pushed the mass to one side. It was like stirring a bowl of spaghetti with a chopstick.

Mark picked up the steaming heart and liver and put them in a pail.

Hal's jaw dropped. "You're going to eat that?"

"It's all good," Mark said.

Bridger whittled away at the hide, which came off in chunks.

"I thought you knew how to do that," Mark stated.

"Just read about how. Never actually skinned an animal," Bridger admitted. "Harder than it looks. Bloody business."

Mark and Hal stared in disbelief at Bridger. Mark blew out a puff of air. "What a fake. I thought you knew your way around the mountains. What did you do before I met you?"

Bridger faced them, his Bowie knife dripping blood at his side. "I was a banker. In Missouri, in charge of loans. They wanted money to get rich on ripping up the land. Mining, timber, housing developments. It was all bad. Got pissed off at all the high-rolling assholes and one day just walked out of the office with a full briefcase."

"Yeah, you said. But…" Hal trailed off speechless.

"I had all these books on survival at home. Like those mountain men on the frontier. I wanted a simpler life." Bridger smiled ruefully. "Didn't reckon on this simple."

"Does anybody…your wife…know where you are?" Hal said.

"I left her and two self-centered kids in her fancy house in the St. Louis 'burbs. Those kids kept me earning the big bucks. Little bastards had to have iPhones, computers, the latest games, and fucking tennis shoes that cost a hundred dollars. The wife wanted the most expensive house in the fanciest neighborhood. Well, now she's got the whole damn shebang. Along with the mortgage."

Hal nodded. "I was gut sick most of the time trying to figure out how to keep my head above water. In some ways, it's a relief just to let it all go."

"Easy, isn't it?"

"Do you have that money with you?" Mark said, too nonchalantly.

"No need to worry about that." Bridger returned to mutilating the deer.

That night they ate meat until they couldn't stuff another bite into their mouths. Mark boiled up the heart. "Be good for breakfast with some fried potatoes."

"Don't make me puke," Hal said.

They lounged on the white plastic chairs, belching and spitting on the pine needles.

"You can't tell me you never ate the heart of one of your little piggies?" Mark scoffed.

Hal curled his lip. "Can't say I did."

"This is heaven," Bridger said, hoisting his heels onto another chair.

"Yeah. A brewski would go down real nice, though." Mark handed his plate and fork to Hal to wash.

In the morning, Hal went out to cut more meat off the carcass and found it crawling with green and black flies. The deer's eyes were yellow from fly eggs. He cut off the shoulders and the second haunch and left the rest on the gut pile or hanging. He threw the meat on the oilcloth-covered table in the tent and said, "Well, that's it. The rest is all fly blown."

"We'll roast this, and it'll keep longer. Tomorrow's the day, so get ready, girls. Hal, can you make some biscuits in that Dutch oven to take with us?"

"I suppose so. My blisters ain't healed yet, though."

"Heal 'em today, 'cause that's all you got."

CHAPTER THIRTEEN

We make good time, passing the riders while they're shaking out their legs, peeing in the bushes, or lying flat on the ground. Most everyone waves and yells a greeting. I take the animals on over the bridge crossing the Sun River, hooves clattering on the thick boards. Later, we stop in an open meadow near the turn-off for White River Pass.

"Just let them graze a while," I call back to Stormy.

She rides up to me, and I cross my leg over the horn and push on Buck's crest to invite her to lower her head to graze.

"The riders are taking their time," she says.

"Probably doing a lot of walking alongside and snapping pictures."

Skip seizes the opportunity to curl up in the shade of a juniper.

"You hungry?" I reach back and lift the flap on my saddlebags.

"Only for you," she says with a slow smile.

"You are bad." I smile back at her. "But good."

"Come down off that horse so I can get my hands on you."

I've never met anyone quite like her. I slide to the ground without too much encouragement. My body has awakened from the deep freeze of grief, and my pounding heart moves hot blood in a rush back to my fingertips and lips. They tingle, alive and warm.

She nuzzles her face into my neck at the junction of my collar, just like Skipper. I'm amused, delighted, and turned on. She gives my lower lip a little bite, then caresses the spot with the edge of her tongue.

"Stormy, I think I hear thunder." I whisper the words into her hair as I press one hand down past the waistband of her jeans into the hollow of her back where her buttocks begin to swell. I draw her firmly against my body, drinking in her sweet smell.

"I felt a jolt of lightning when you kissed me." Stormy's soft laugh resonates through my body.

We are both wrong. It's the sound of hooves. Thank God for Skip. She jumps up out of her nest and gives one short bark.

We look up to see the riders appear with Jess in the lead. They hold up while we gather the string back for the trail.

"Having fun yet?" I call out.

A chorus of agreement comes back to me, and I see smiles on nearly every woman's face. I note the one exception—two, if you count Jess—is the North Carolina woman, Roseanne. She looks cranky and tired.

"We're not far from the turn-off for the pass," I call out. "Over the top, it's all downhill."

"These mountains are spectacular. I had no idea they would be so impressive," Barbara says with a bright, exhilarated smile. Her camera is hanging around her neck at the ready.

Stormy and I get the string lined out, and we're on the trail again. The pack-string knows this route by now and is eager for the feed bins at the end.

We have to work through a brushy patch, packs scraping at the fine branches. I remember a good-sized huckleberry patch on this side of the mountain. This part always makes me a little nervous, looking for bear. Once we break free of the brush, I glance around carefully and spy a grizzly off a comfortable way to the right. He's sitting on his rump, belly wide and full, using his long claws to rake the berries straight from the branches into his mouth. He's annoyed at being interrupted from his fat-building.

I call back to Stormy to warn the others. Women grab for their cameras and cell phones when the dude train clears the brush. At the sight of so many riders, the bear moves away, fading into the scrub. Excited chatter wafts up to us as we begin the long switchbacks to the top.

The horses rear up to take the high rock shelves along the trail, lurching up the steps. A few shrieks can be heard from riders.

We cross the divide, the wall off to our right, broken but still impressive. Wind swoops around as I set my hat a little deeper. The trail drops abruptly, horses scrambling on the scree. On our left, the cliff plummets to the waterfall of the south fork of the White River.

I can never go by this spot without my stomach clutching and my heart shattering into so many parts it takes a concerted effort to bring them back to whole again. This is where Ginger and her horse plunged over the edge to her death. No roadside white crosses mark this place, just the sharp edges of my heart.

I draw in deep breaths, letting the air out so slowly, I can feel my lungs deflate. All my attention is on the scrub growth, stunted trees, and the receding lines of undulating mountains, growing mistier to the distant west. I seek any place to aim my eyes rather than the drop-off to the river far below.

After I had mounted up at the rest stop, I pulled Jess and Karen aside and told them to keep the riders well to the right on the loose scree slope just over the pass. And why. Karen nodded, remembering the story I told her at our first meeting.

The riders have faded back, taking the trail more slowly than Stormy or I do, but they can't get lost now.

I catch a whiff of smoke as we near camp. Some backpackers out this far, I think, maybe taking advantage of the comfort of a stove and the wall tent. I slow down and get more cautious. I have a clear view of the camp at a bend in the trail, so I stop my horse, holding up my hand for Stormy to halt. I dismount, then tie Buck to a tree branch and pull my binoculars out of the saddlebags. Backpackers often bivouac at an empty outfitter camp where there are too many amenities to pass up. I hope our food isn't one of them.

I can see smoke coming from the wall tent stove, and I spot a partial deer carcass hanging from a tree with a pile of cans outside the cook tent. This doesn't look good. Some poacher has taken over our camp.

If there's trouble, I want to be ready for it. I'm filled with dread. Well, the rifle doesn't need to be in the middle of any confrontation. I unstrap my rifle with the scabbard and move into the trees. I find a big fir where I can place it high enough to stay dry and not be seen. For quicker access, I unbuckle the saddlebag holding my revolver, thinking the rifle will be useless at close quarters, anyway.

I walk back along the pack string to Stormy. "Probably some backpackers are playing mountain man. Squatting on the camp. Did you mark where I put the rifle? That tall tree?"

She nods and asks what I've seen. I tell her, adding, "Our group probably took a break at the top, so we've got a little time to suss the situation."

I lean against Stormy's horse, touching her leg with my shoulder, and straighten a small wind twist in her horse's black mane. The mare turns to nose my pockets.

We ride down toward camp, cautious and slow.

Two rough-looking men appear from the tent, one in buckskins and the other in camo. Stormy takes the string over to the tie-up rails, and I ride up to the interlopers as a third man exits the tent flap. He's chunky and has a beard.

"Fellers, we've got guests," the man in camo says. He rests his hand on a pistol holster strapped to his hip.

"It's those same guys." The bearded man eyes us.

"Those ain't guys. Ladies come calling," buckskin man says with a leer.

"This camp is occupied, so you fellows need to leave," I state.

"You bet it's occupied, honey." Camo man walks over toward the packhorses. "What did you bring us? Something good to eat?"

Stormy doesn't answer. She's busy tending to the horses like he's not even there. Smart of her. Whatever happens, we must secure the horses, because if there's some crisis there's no way we can deal with them. I ride up, dismount, and say, with more boldness than I feel, "We've got work to do, so stand back."

We go about our job unpacking the stock, releasing them into the corral. My mind is racing. This could get ugly. How do you get rid of three renegade men?

I unsaddle Buck and lead her into the corral. I can hear the women on the trail, light chatter, the click of horseshoes. There's still time. I lead Buck to the far side of the corral, closest to the trail, dash across to the pole fence, and climb over. Behind me someone shouts, "Hey!"

I keep going, angling up through the firs to the trail.

"Stop!" A shot rings out, slapping through the trees to my right. I reach the trail, stand in the middle of it with my arms raised, and yell, "Go back! Turn around and go back."

Jess's face tells me she has got it. She whips her horse around, bumping into Roseanne's horse, which is following too close. "Turn around! Now," she shouts.

Someone grabs my arm, twisting it up behind with a shove, forcing me to my knees. "Shut up!" he demands.

My shoulder is on fire. "Run!" I scream out.

This earns me a kick to my hip, and he jerks my arm up harder. Pain sears my shoulder, and all my breath comes out in a grunt.

Women are trying to turn their reluctant horses, which see the packhorses and know this is the end of the trail and a long day's work. The back of the line is utter confusion, horses milling in a clump.

Karen yells, "What's wrong?"

"Turn around and ride back." Jess is trying to haze the women's horses back up the trail.

The guy with the gun appears to my right and points it straight up, letting off a shot. He screams, "Stay right there. Nobody's going anywhere."

Roseanne's horse rears, and she hits the ground.

The guy in buckskins leaves me to grab the bridle of Jess's horse. The heavy guy runs up to Roseanne and says to her, "Are you hurt?" He helps her up and brushes some pine needles off her back.

"No, I don't think so," Roseanne answers in a daze.

The guy with the gun steps to one side and starts issuing orders. "Get off your horses and lead them down here." He waves the gun toward camp, and then he points it straight at me. "And you, stay where I can see you."

At the end of the line, there is confusion and disbelief. Karen rides forward. "What's going on here?"

"Get off your horses. Now!" The camo guy's voice is high and thin.

The women dismount slowly and make their way down the trail past the guy with the gun.

"That's a mutilated deer," one of the women says. She's the gray-haired one from Seattle. "Taken out of season, I might add."

Luci sneers. "Disgusting. Absolutely covered with flies."

The women have stopped to stare at the horror of the carcass, awareness of the danger from these men sinking to the bottom of their guts.

"Jesus, look at all these ladies coming to visit," the buckskin-clad man says, a big smile on his face. He turns and shoves me forward.

Jess is pissed. "What's this bullshit?" She is the last to climb off her horse and confronts the guy with the gun. I admire her courage, but think it might be a touch unwise. "You guys are going to have to clear out. This is our—"

She doesn't get the words out because camo guy slaps her across her face. She hits the dirt from the impact. Jess looks up at the guy, shaking her head in an effort to clear it.

The big guy steps forward. "Don't hurt her, Mark."

"Stay out of this. They'll all do as I say or one of them will get hurt. I'll guarantee it."

I glance back along the women and see fear and disbelief. While the focus is on Jess, I remove my saddlebags from the back of my saddle and take them into the corral to stash them in the feeders. I'm going to need this gun.

Karen ties her horse to the rail and approaches the men. "What is it you want? We could spare three horses if that will send you on your way."

"No, we can't." Jess stands up. "They're not taking my horses."

"Be quiet, Jess." Karen continues, speaking reasonably to the men. "We don't want any trouble."

I can see the three men are considering this. One of them says, "Mark, we could ride down to where the canoe is, crossing the river would be a lot easier."

"Shut up, Hal. How are you going to do that when neither you nor Bridger know how to ride?"

"Can't be that hard. Maybe we could get three gentle—"

"Forget it."

Karen tries to defuse the situation. "These are dude horses suitable for beginners. The horses are already saddled, and there are saddlebags for your gear."

I realize too that this is the quickest, easiest way to get rid of these guys. I say to Jess, "Pick out the three easiest horses to manage."

"No! We aren't taking horses. They look tired, and it's late." Mark is clearly the leader. Hal looks disappointed.

Bridger steps up. "How're we supposed to manage this many women? Have you thought of that, Mark?"

"We'll tie up this one." He motions to Jess. "Keep her in the tent with us. Any of you act up and she dies. Understand?"

"Can't we get a pretty one? How 'bout that blonde?"

My body goes cold. I know who they mean.

"This one's the troublemaker," Mark says.

I breathe out in relief. Small comfort.

Mark grabs Jess's arm and jerks her toward the tent. Suddenly, Skipper leaps forward and grabs the man's leg. He lashes out with one booted foot, and she takes a couple of steps back, low growls rumbling from her body with menacing hackles raised.

Mark raises his gun.

I step between them. "Leave her alone." I wave Skip back, and she retreats. "This dog is trained to warn against bears. You kill her, and there's no way to know if there are bears around."

Mark lowers his gun. "Keep the damned dog away from me, or he's dead."

I slap my leg to call Skip to my side. Her hackles are still up, but she comes to me with one eye on the men.

"Let's get these horses unsaddled," I say with as much calm as I can muster.

Stormy is there to take horses from the women, who are too stunned to act. An air of unreality settles over us. Or maybe too much reality.

Chapter Fourteen

G o to your tents and no funny business," Mark says.

I nearly laugh, the tension is so high. I didn't think anyone actually said that. He must have seen too many matinee movies as a kid.

"I have to finish dealing with the stock," I tell him, leading the last horse into the corrals. I heft a bag of pellets, Stormy getting another, and we dump them into the feeders. With Karen's help, women are gathering up their sleeping bags and personal packs from the heap of things we took off the packhorses. As they collect their things, they move toward the tents.

"What are we going to do with all the supplies we just packed in?" Stormy says.

"I'm not about to haul the food into the cook tent for those guys. The rest will just have to sit there until we get this worked out."

"You mean when they leave?"

"Hopefully in the morning."

I call Skipper to my side. We gather up our bedrolls and packs. I cross my fingers the air mattresses are still where we left them in the sleeping tents. I stuff a bag of dried fruit down the front of my jeans and hand Stormy a bag of granola bars.

I whisper to Stormy, "Let's meet in the middle tent. Lift the back flap where it's tied to the floor. Tell Karen, if you can. We've got to talk this out."

❖

I can see Stormy head-to-head with Karen. She nods, and then she ducks into the center tent.

We go to our respective tents: Kamau, Luci, and Roseanne with me; Rachel, Sue, and Mike with Stormy. Candace and Barbara will go in with Karen. And Jess, when we get her back.

I rotate my shoulder, rubbing the pain. A bad business, nothing funny about it.

I settle Skip on my bedroll and unwrap a couple of peanut granola bars I've slipped into my pocket for her. Better than nothing. She agrees, wolfing them down.

"You're so brave," I tell her. "But I don't want to lose you, so no more funny business." I ruffle her ears. "I'll dig out your dog food as soon as I can."

When Stormy and I had set up camp, we'd left four air mattresses inside each tent. Only one remains in here. I give it to Roseanne. "They must have taken three. I'll get two more to replace them."

Luci frowns. "That's not right. You can't sleep on the hard ground."

I give her a slow smile. "I'll be okay. Won't be the first time, but I'll get some saddle pads to cushion my old bones."

I lift the tent flap to see where the men are, and then I saunter out to the rail where we left the gear. Raised, angry voices come through the canvas walls of the cook tent.

I figure they are pretty distracted and creep closer to hear what's going on.

"You've really gotten us into a fix now, Mark. What the hell are we going to do?"

"Shut up! I'm thinking."

"Those women didn't do anything to us. Let's leave in the morning before we hurt somebody. We can take those horses."

"I sure don't want to go to prison. I can have the good life with what I've got," a different voice put in.

"Don't worry. I sure as fuck don't want to either."

I've heard enough and am grateful for the dusk and shadows as I find Skip's dog food. I gather up five of the thick felt packsaddle pads with a couple of wool saddle blankets. I toss three into my tent and place the others outside the center tent. I call to the women inside. "I'm going to need two air mattresses in trade for these saddle pads."

In a moment, two mattresses slide through the slit in the tent. I grab them and go back to make up my bedroll with folded blankets at my feet for Skipper.

Luci and Kamau are reluctant to take the air mattresses. "You've had a hard day, too."

"Yeah, but I've done this before."

After the men's voices quiet down, I douse the battery lantern in our tent and tell Skip to stay. We sneak under the back flap. I send the other women in to be with Karen and then scratch on Stormy's tent. "Come on," I whisper.

They all dive for the food Stormy and I show up with. "I'm starved," says Sue. "I thought we wouldn't have anything to eat. Very clever of you to grab this."

"Guess it will do until morning. Not what we'd planned for your first night's dinner."

While we devour the stash, I tell them what I overheard.

"So, these unsavory men are all worried about being caught and sent to prison?" Karen says.

"Sounds like it. That makes them desperate." I frown,

looking around at the women's faces. "This is one helluva mess."

I tell them about my rifle hidden in the tree and the gun in the saddlebags. "I sure hope we don't have to use them," I add.

"I'm not comfortable with all the guns or the mentality of thinking they'll help us," Barbara says.

Mike puts her two cents worth in. "Better having them and not using them than wishing we did."

Rachel snorts. "Hell. I'm not comfortable with any part of it. You've got the right idea, Karen. They are on their way someplace, let's just encourage that."

"I'll second that," Barbara says. "No shoot-outs, just sacrifice three of our horses."

"There'll be less to pack out anyway," I say. "We can probably fit all your personal gear and everything we need on fewer horses. Stormy and I will have to come back in anyway to break down the camp and bring out the tents and the rest of the gear. We can bring in extra packhorses."

"With any luck, they'll leave in the morning. Jess is in a bad situation. I'm so worried they'll harm her. Wish we could do something to help her." Karen is in anguish. "I'm so sorry, everyone, that our trip—"

"Oh, no. It's not your fault." Sue and Candace hold her in their arms and soothe her.

We freeze at the sound of a high scream. Jess.

I imagine everyone feels as helpless and furious as I do.

"There are eleven of us. We can overpower them," Mike says. "Let's go now."

"I'll second that," Kamau adds.

"No! Somebody will get hurt. It's a big risk," Stormy says, holding up one hand.

"Please. Let's not rush into anything. They might even hurt her worse, kill her, and they'll be watching and ready for us." Karen paces three short steps and stares off in the direction of Jess's scream.

I ball my fist and slam it against my thigh. "I feel so helpless. I've got to do something."

With a calm I envy, Karen says, "No, Miles, stay. I agree it is horrible, but we'll have to try to deal with the aftermath. To try to save Jess right now is to risk her being hurt worse, and whoever rides to the rescue suffering as well."

"If we get an advantage, who's with me?" I study the women around me. I count on Kamau and Mike. "That's three of us."

"Really, count me in, too," another voice says. It's Candace, who raises her fist. "Honestly, it's women power."

"Yeah!" Mike punches the air.

"Oh, honey, don't do anything rash." Sue puts her arm around Mike, leaning into her.

"I say, fuck 'em. Get them if we can." Kamau has her knuckles at her hips, legs planted slightly apart.

"Very butch," says Candace.

"I'm not a butch. I'm a boi."

"You mean trans?" Candace hesitates. "You spell that b-o-i, right?"

"That's right. All that need to gender-slot people is just too U-Haul."

"U-Haul?" Luci's amused smile adds a question mark. "What on earth do you mean?"

"You know. The happy couple moves in together after the first date and makes a nuclear family. Not my game."

"What game do you play?" Luci does those little sexy moves with her body that makes it obvious what game she wants to play.

"God! I'm so tired I can't think of anything exerting right

now." Roseanne sighs, obviously very uncomfortable with where this is heading.

Karen says, "Let's join in a prayer circle to restore harmony to our camp and protect us."

I want to duck out, not being one for led prayer groups, but can't separate myself from this bunch right now. I'm all for it if prayer will help us out of this mess. We sit on the canvas floor in a rough circle, not actually touching and definitely not holding hands or swaying. That's a plus.

Karen sits with her hands on her knees, palms up. She hums a deep throbbing sound then speaks. "Hold us in the light. Protect Jess from this ravaging attack. Take the pain and fear to the river on the wind and send it over the round stones to the sea."

My mind is racing from one scattered thought to the next. I try to send the huge chunks of worry and fear into the flowing White River to be carried away. In spite of myself, I feel an enveloping calm extending out to the women sitting on either side of me.

Karen rises to her feet, helps Luci up, and says, "Thank you for all of your presences. We can do it together. Turn in now, and maybe things will get better tomorrow. I'll talk them into taking the horses."

"Seems like the best way out of this," I agree.

We exit under the back edge of the tent, and Barbara looks up. "Look at that!"

"What?" I say with an edge of alarm.

"The sky. It's full of stars. And there's the Milky Way. Oh, my God! I've never seen it like this."

I smile and say, "No moon yet. And no city lights to dull them."

Rachel's deep laugh comes from right behind me. "I am

usually in bed by the time it gets really dark, but I see them sometimes in the morning."

Mike and Sue are just as awed by the canopy of sky. Mike says, "When I was a kid at summer camp, I remember lying on the grass just staring up at the stars. It was the first time I felt how insignificant I was. All my problems as a twelve-year-old were swept away."

Candace says, "Really, I wish they'd sweep our problems away right now."

Barbara cranes her head back. "Living in Seattle, I forget they're out there. So crisp and bright."

"Yeah," Kamau agrees. "Puts everything in perspective."

Luci slips her arms around Kamau from behind. "Sure does."

Roseanne moves toward our tent and breaks the spell.

Stormy comes with me, and we lie close all night. Lovemaking is the last thing on our minds.

We've come to a wall—not the one we expected, but one just as formidable.

In the morning, Stormy and I go to the corrals and separate the pack from the riding animals with the hope I won't have to use any feed pellets. If I can sort out three horses for the men to use and run the rest out to grass, I will be happy. I'm worried about having enough feed to last through this nightmare. My saddlebags are still in the corner of the feeder, slightly chewed. I remove the gun in its holster, tucking it between some corner poles, and take the bags back to my saddle.

I think about sliding the gun under my coat but decide it is still too early for that sort of confrontation.

I hear the beautiful singing sound of some musical instrument. I walk over to Stormy and whisper, "What is that lovely sound?"

Karen appears, walking slowly, mindfully one step at a

time, with a brass bowl in her hands, running one finger around the rim.

"It's a Buddhist prayer bowl," Stormy says softly.

The other women are beginning to appear from the tents, some making their way to the outhouse. We are wary as a bunch of cats.

Smoke rises from the cook tent. One of the guys, I think his name is Hal, comes out. He can't meet my eyes.

I approach him. "We want Jess returned to us. Plus we're going to have to cook some food for us, you know? We've had a hard day yesterday and nothing to eat." I try to sound reasonable instead of begging.

He goes back into the tent without answering.

On the way back to our tents, I meet Karen. "Try again to get them to leave. We've got to fix something to eat, and the horses are getting restless. I should be running them out to graze."

"I'm scared," she admits. "I'll go talk with them. Come with me, will you, Miles?"

We go over to the cook tent. I yell out, "Hey."

All three men come out. "What do you want?" the guy in camo demands.

"How is Jess?" Karen says. "Have you hurt—?"

"She's having the time of her life." Mark smirks.

"We want you to leave. The horses are rested. I urge you to take three and clear out. The Rangers are looking for you." Karen sounds so centered and calm.

Hal says, "Look, guys, I think she has a point. We don't want to be sitting ducks here if some feds show up."

Mark stares at Karen, his eyes narrow.

Bridger says, "Let's take the horses. I don't fancy crossing that river on foot."

"We'll think about it." Mark turns to go back in the tent.

"I'll have to run the horses upriver to graze this morning. There's not enough feed to keep them in the corrals while you make up your minds." I hope this is the push they need to make a decision.

"Turn them loose?" Bridger looks stunned. "Just out there?"

"I'll go get them when you've made a decision about when you're leaving." I wait to see what their reaction is.

"How do we know you'll come back?" Mark is put up against making a choice. He wavers.

"There's no place else to go. Driving the horses north to graze is a dead end, eventually." I take a deep breath. "We have to have Jess back and access to the kitchen or it's no deal."

Mark laughs. "What deal? We didn't make no deal." He hesitates then says, "Three of you can have fifteen minutes in the kitchen. Hal, you and Bridger bring all the saddles in here."

"I have to have my saddle and one for another wrangler."

Karen says, "What about Jess?"

"Oh, hell, take her. I'm sick of her. She whines all the time." He goes into the tent and reappears, shoving Jess ahead of him. Jess staggers over to us, her shirt ripped and her face devastated. We gather her in our arms.

I stare at them, my eyes narrowed. "Damn you!"

"Don't get mouthy, or you'll be next, you stringy hermaphrodite."

Karen grabs my arm and pulls me away.

We lead Jess to our tent. Women come out to encircle her. Jess is furious. I'm relieved to see her spirit is not broken. "I'm going to kill him." Her face is contorted with hatred.

Karen says, "We're going to get rid of them, Jess." She holds her close and pets her forehead. "I'm so sorry you went through that. We all wanted to rescue you and felt so frustrated that we couldn't, that we could put you in greater danger."

Barbara asks, "I know you've been terribly violated, but are you physically hurt?"

Jess bursts into tears. "Mark raped me while the others watched. They wouldn't, or couldn't rape me, but they did nothing to stop Mark. I'm sore and feel filthy."

"Mike." I call to her as the one nearest. "There are sun showers, those black bags, laid out in the sun. Stormy and I filled them before we rode back to Benchmark. Rig one up in the shower stall so Jess can bathe."

She gives me a solemn nod and ducks under the tent flap.

Sue comes up to Jess and takes both her hands, "I am so sorry you experienced that terrible night." Her eyes through the thick lenses are swimming with tears.

Barbara says, "Miles, I want us to figure out a way to get Jess back to town. She needs to see a doctor and be checked for sexually transmitted diseases."

"Oh, no," Jess says so reasonably. "I just need to bathe." Her face turns red. She chokes on her words and covers her face with her open hands.

"Is your vagina torn or bruised?" Barbara is gentle, her voice soft and soothing.

Jess nods, her lips pressed tight together. "I've been bleeding some, down there."

"We can figure out a way to slip you out of here. One of us will go with you. We'll work out the details tonight." Barbara checks with me, and I nod.

Karen says, "Right now, we need three women to get into the tent and cook up food for all of us. They're only giving us fifteen minutes. No, not you, Stormy. You and Miles need to saddle your horses and run the stock out to grass."

"All of them?" Stormy says.

"For now," I say.

Karen looks around. "Who will come with me to cook?"

Sue takes off her glasses and cleans them on her shirttail. She nods. Roseanne steps up. "Me too." They head down to fix us food. Stormy and I catch our mounts and lead them over to the tie-up rail. I sling my saddle up over the wool pad.

Bridger and Hal approach to commandeer the saddles, following Mark's orders.

Hal nonchalantly tries to lift one of the stock saddles, says, "Shit. This thing weighs a ton. How do those girls lift them onto the horses?"

Stormy tosses words over her shoulder. "Because we aren't girls."

Bridger says, "Just get them into the tent." He winks at Hal. "Like keys to the car, remember?"

We watch them drag the saddles, one by one, across the dirt toward the tent. Stormy shakes her head, rolls her eyes, and then she lays the pad on her horse and swings her saddle up, easy as you please. I smile for the first time in hours. We get ready quick before they change their volatile minds.

Sue comes over to give us some canned black bean burritos and two bananas. "Here's something to tide you over."

"Thanks. Looks mighty good."

She says, "It's a total wreck in there. They've dumped cans all over the floor and garbage is everywhere. Pigs."

I shake my head and shove breakfast into my saddlebags. "Which one is the lead mare?" I ask Stormy.

"That one with the white sock over her right front knee and a bald face."

I ease up to the mare and put a halter on her, then buckle a bell strap high on her neck. "Can you lead her? Skip and I will push the rest along."

I open the gate, we mount up and whoop the horses out toward the river. Just before the crossing, I get Skip to jump into the saddle in front of me so she won't have to fight the deep water. On the far side, I let Skip slip to the ground. The riding horses are following the packhorses, and they know rich grass is ahead. The trail borders the clear rushing water, slightly uphill between tall firs. Centuries of evergreen needles muffle the horse's steel shoes. We move silently through the dark trees to burst out into the sunshine in a cliff-rimmed valley.

Chapter Fifteen

The mare moves out on the rope behind Stormy, her cowbell ringing cheerfully. I mean to take them far up the valley, beyond where any stock have grazed from previous trips this summer, where it's just a little hard to round them up. We pass the gladiator rock outcrop and move into a large meadow with knee-high grass. I call to Stormy to lead the bay mare in a large circle to stop the forward movement of the herd, and then to remove her halter.

The mules and horses mill around for a minute before attacking the grass. The sound of their teeth ripping the grass off is actually audible. One horse drops to his knees, rolling, feet in the air, grunting with pleasure. A scattered few join in, scratching their backs.

Stormy and I ride off to one side, dismount, and watch the horses settle in. The sound of the river rushing behind us is soothing. My brain feels tight, like it's filled with concrete.

I drop Buck's bit so she can eat while we're standing there, and Stormy follows suit. The horses are ravenous for the grass. Even fifteen minutes of grazing will help the feed situation for our two riding horses. Back at camp, we can hobble ours, then turn them out on the grass around the tents.

My stomach's growling, and I lift my saddlebag flap to get out a banana and the burrito.

"I can't help but think about what Jess went through," Stormy says softly.

"Barbara is right. We have to figure out some way to get Jess out of here as soon as possible." I focus on the herd of grazing horses, trying to imagine some way to get two horses and saddles to use for Jess and a companion.

"I feel so guilty we didn't do anything to stop it." Stormy takes two steps away and paces back to me. She hammers her fists at her side.

"I'm sure we all do. Hard to stand up to men with guns. I've been wracking my brains to think of how to get rid of them if they don't take Karen's suggestion."

"We could kill them. You have your gun, and I could sneak back and get the rifle."

"A shoot-out would leave at least one of us hurt. I don't know—we've got to be more clever than that." A crystal-clear scene of Jane advising me on reaching the men's inner light came full-blown into my mind. Her Quaker belief was that we have the ability and the responsibility to find that place in each of us that is good, kind, and not be stuck on the surface evil when we encounter that. The vision had the power to make me believe in ghosts. I took a deep breath and rubbed my hand over my eyes. "Karen's idea for them to take horses is the best one. I think she's made inroads on convincing them."

"Bastards! I hate to help them in any way." Stormy slaps her palm with the rein ends.

"Mark's the wild hare. The other two look to him, though. If we could somehow..." I focused on the high clouds and closed my eyes. "Oh, hell, I can't imagine any scenario that might work." I reach down and pull the grass seeds off a long stem. Skipper watches me and gives a little whine. She knows something is not right.

Stormy puts her arm around me and rests her head against

my shoulder. She nuzzles her face against my wool vest. "You'll come up with something."

I glance at the white burn scars on my wrist. I got out of that jam. Maybe I can help us get out of this.

"It's good to be away from that horror, even for a short time," she says, lips moving against my vest.

"Yes, but we'll have to go back soon. Eat."

Stormy obligingly gets out her food and wolfs it down after a bite or two. We stand there for a while longer. It feels so good to have Stormy in the shelter of my arms.

When she crinkles up the wrapper, I glance at my watch and pull away from her warmth. We replace the bridles on the horses, and I woodenly mount Buck to turn her back to camp. A few horses try to follow us, and I motion Skip to haze them back to the others.

In camp, Mark is sitting on a white plastic chair with the gun resting in his lap. "Took you long enough."

Stormy and I halt our horses near him. I nod over to the disaster they've made of the deer. "You guys have to do something about that."

"Why? Does it offend you?" he says with a sneer.

"It'll draw bear. And fast."

That wipes the smile from his face and makes him sit up. "Do something about it. Hal, you go help her."

Hal curls his lip. "It stinks."

"Get a tarp," I tell him, "the small one from the corner by the tools. And a shovel."

He does as I say, already having been ordered to by Mark. I tie Buck on the corral poles, then spread the tarp by the gut pile. The smell is intense.

I say to Stormy, "I'll need your horse."

She raises her eyebrows, and I explain. "I'll need to ride her while I pack this mess away on Buck."

"Can I help?"

"No. This is a one-person job once I get it loaded."

Hal is just standing there with no idea what to do.

"Lower the carcass and drag it here." I start shoveling the guts onto the tarp, stirring up the flies, which form a cloud all around, walking with their tiny feet all over my face, inside my nostrils. I raise my bandanna to cover my mouth and nose. When all the deer parts are on the tarp, I say to Hal, "Get some more rope. That thinner nylon cord." He wanders back to the tent, rubbing his face.

I fold the tarp in an envelope over the remains of the deer, and when Hal returns, I lash it tight. I lead Buck over, drop the reins, and she stands while Hal and I lift the package onto her back and tie it in place. The sound of the trapped flies buzzing frantically inside the tarp makes my stomach curl around the banana.

"Where you going with that?" Hal wipes his hands on his jeans.

"As far from camp as I can get. While I'm gone, sprinkle wood ashes over the ground here."

"You can do that. Or one of the other ladies. I'm done."

"Bastard," I mutter under my breath.

When all is ready, I go to Stormy. "Can you watch Skip? I don't want her to come with me."

"Sure thing." She reaches down to pet Skip, who is eyeing me, waiting for a signal.

"Stay here." I wave my hand down. She moves her front legs forward and drops to the ground, her nose resting against her legs, eyeing me.

I put the bell mare's halter on Buck, mount up Stormy's bay, and cross the river, riding west along the White. I remember the guys saying something about going out this way. It really is the only way other than White River Pass to leave camp. With any luck, I can attract bear someplace where there's dense cover right along the trail. A bear trap for the men.

I ride about an hour from camp. The trail follows the river close enough to hear the rippling water cross the rocks. We travel high through dense woods, then eventually near where the trail crosses the river again.

This little mare of Stormy's is a pleasure to ride, light and responsive. Makes me think about adding some Arabian blood to my herd. Most ranchers disdain Arabians as being flighty or just pretty lawn ornaments.

Dense alders grow along the water's edge, and I figure this is a good place. I dismount, tie the horses to a couple of saplings, and pull the carcass off Buck. It lands with a squishy thunk. She holds steady, as I knew she would.

I drag the tarp into the alders and untie the packaged remains. The flies are angry at their confinement and burst into the air around me when I unfold the tarp. After I roll the mess out onto the ground at the base of the alders, I'm humbled by its devastation.

I take the tarp to the river and rinse it off best I can, shake it, roll it tight, and tie it behind my saddle with the saddle strings.

Chapter Sixteen

Back in camp, I pull the tack off the horses, hobble them, and turn them loose to pick at the grass around the tents. Karen and Roseanne are at the cook tent trying to put together lunch. For some odd reason, Hal is helping them by gathering firewood.

Mark is lounging in a nearby chair with a sneer on his face as he watches Hal. "You trying to suck up to the ladies, Hal?"

Hal looks down, and he actually blushes. "They're having a hard time of it, Mark. You could go easier on them, give them a little more time to prepare food."

"Forget it. No fuckin' way. Them's the rules."

I turn quickly away so the lowlife can't see my smile. The big dogs in the pack always forget they aren't the smartest.

Karen spies me watching and waves me over. "I'm cooking up a soup, but fifteen minutes isn't enough time to cook beans or rice, so our protein levels will suffer. The men are eating all the canned beans and peanut butter, and have eaten all the cheese, so we are really limited in our diet."

"So? It's all ours now," Mark says.

Karen turns her gaze to Mark, her eyes appearing almost rectangular slits like a lizard. He shifts uncomfortably, looking away at the tops of mountains.

I remember the big griddle at the bottom of the stack of pans, lift it out, and tell Karen, "I'll make that happen. Bring a pot and what you need to cook."

Outside the small tent, downwind of the other two, I dig away the duff and leaves to make a fire pit. Stormy comes over, sees what I'm doing, and we clear back anything that can burn to about five feet. We gather rocks big enough to stay stable and arrange them with an opening to the west, to the prevailing wind.

While this is in process, Karen and Roseanne return with a lunch soup, assembled from cans of vegetables and half-cooked pasta. Karen is carrying a bag each of pinto beans and rice. With triumph, she holds up one onion. Roseanne has a small bag of seasoning chipotle, dried celery and onion flakes, tomato and vegetable stock bullion cubes. She says, "This ought to make dinner more palatable."

Roseanne glances back toward the cook tent. "Hal was very helpful, wasn't he?"

Karen uncharacteristically grunts, and then she sets the pot with the soup down beside the fire pit. "This soup could stand some more cooking."

"Almost ready," I tell her.

Bridging the rocks with the griddle, I add more flat rocks along the edges and create a chimney hole to the east end of the stove. I stand and smile at Karen. "Should work pretty good."

"I'll say." Hal takes us off guard. His arms are full of wood, and he has some newspaper for fire starter. He smiles at Roseanne, and she returns it with a swing of her hips and a little pat to her hair. I stare at her, speechless.

Hal dumps the wood by our little stove and lays the paper on top. "Not much paper around, but this'll start a few fires." He looks me square in the face. "Smart of you to put this together. I'll talk to Mark. He won't mind you doing this."

I take a breath to tell him I don't care if Mark approves or not and feel Karen's calm hand on my shoulder.

"Thank you, Hal. Perhaps in the morning, you can take horses and continue on your trip." Karen smiles and sets the pan on the griddle.

I lean over to lay the fire and hear his footsteps receding. In a moment, Roseanne returns to the tent.

"Did you catch that little number between Roseanne and Hal?" I say softly to Karen.

She gently laughs. "Consorting with the enemy?"

"She can't be interested in him."

"I never claimed all the women on the trip would be lesbians. I advertise in women's journals and magazines. Generally, it is mostly lesbians who are attracted to an all-women trip."

"Roseanne was actually simpering." I shove a short piece of wood on the flames devouring the handful of tiny dead fir branches. "It means we can't trust her or make any plans around her."

"Oh, I don't think we need to go that far," Karen says.

"Something to think about. If I'm noticing this budding romance, so is everyone else. It'll make for some hard feelings." I stand and brush the duff off my jeans. "Well, I stink after that deer episode."

I go find Stormy. "Do you want to take a shower with me? I filled a black bag up this morning and it might just be lukewarm about now."

She grins. "I'll get my soap and be right with you."

"Like, can I join you? I honestly reek."

I whip around at Candace's voice. Her smile is seductive, inviting. She is removing her barrettes like she's stripping.

Stormy pushes past her carrying her towel. "I don't think so."

My eyes crinkle at her.

The shower is pretty makeshift, built out of poles with a privacy screen to the cook-tent side. We use the rope to sling the sun shower high enough to get a trickle of warm water. We peel off our clothes, hang them on bushes, and proceed to soap each other in all the right places. My hair is easy to wash, but hers still has soap in it when the water runs out.

"Hold on a sec, and I'll get the other bag." I towel off, jerk on my jeans and a T-shirt, and retrieve the second bag, slinging it up high.

Rachel appears beside me, "Sounds like you two are having too much fun. Any water left?"

"Come on in." Stormy turns the clamp to shut the water off, grabs her towel, and steps aside.

"Guess we were being rowdy." I wink at Stormy, pulling on my socks and boots.

She groans. "Oh, God, that felt good."

I hand her the towel and refrain from touching her breasts. Being good can be so hard. For something else to do, I take the first shower bag and refill it with cold water from the spring, then put it out in the sun.

Out of the corner of my eye, I spy movement back in the trees. Not a deer. A creepy sensation slips up my spine. I walk over and flush Bridger from the underbrush. "You've been spying on us. Get out!"

He slinks off, trying for a last bit of bravado. "We own you."

"That's what you think, you piece of shit."

"Watch your mouth, lesbo."

Both Rachel and Stormy are shocked they've been exposed to his leering eyes.

"I'm rigging a new shower behind our tents," I tell them.

"I'll help," Stormy says, lacing her boots.

We cut a pole and tie it between two trees. The tents do a good job of blocking it from the cook tent area, and it is exposed enough that we can see anyone approaching. We string up three pack manties to give extra privacy.

Talk about the spying event runs hot.

"Never could understand what men get out of watching naked women," Rachel says. "I mean, I admire a woman's body, but…ye Gods. What Bridger did is a form of rape."

"They pay for peep shows." Sue shakes her head. "Go figure."

Later, we all gather around for our first hot lunch. Somehow, Karen has put together a very tasty dish. Afterward, I add the two-pound bag of pinto beans to the pot with a tablespoon of dried onion, pour water over the works, and set it on the griddle top.

"Stormy, can you assign wood gatherers to keep this fire going all afternoon?"

"Sure thing." She calls out the names of three women. "Can you be the first crew? Good. Go as far from camp as possible and break off the dry limbs from the fir trees."

Luci says, "Go out there? Into the forest? There are animals out there. What if I get lost?"

I realize this is true wilderness for many of these women. A big unknown, full of scary challenges, like for people used to the country to go into a large city and cope with the confusion and chaos of traffic and subways and people very different from them. "I'll come too, and everyone can stay within sight of each other."

Once the pile of dry limbs is built, it all seems easier for the city women to go back out for more wood.

Karen goes down to the tent for some carrots and cans of tomatoes. We don't have to worry about the men gobbling those up. I'm chopping carrots when I hear laughter. Hal and

Roseanne are walking hand in hand down toward the river. He leans near her and whispers something in her ear. Roseanne glows, a woman in love.

Karen may not see this budding romance as an issue, but I sure do. I can tell others have a problem with it, too. Especially Jess. We'll have to bring it out in the open, preferably with Roseanne present.

The beans send up a heavenly aroma in the late afternoon. Women begin appearing from the tents to sit in a circle around the fire.

Kamau laughs. "I'm actually drooling. For beans! Go figure."

Soon we're all gathered except Roseanne. Rachel is the first to speak. "I suppose we've all witnessed the romance going on."

Kamau and Luci look up quickly with guilty expressions. Rachel laughs. "No. Not you two."

"She means our resident turncoat," Mike says.

"Oh, come on." Stormy takes up a stick and jabs the ground. "You can't help who you're attracted to."

"That's for sure." Candace shoots me a glance. "I mean, really."

"But Hal's a murderer." Sue pushes her glasses up with one finger. The thick glass adds intensity to her dark eyes.

"Here she comes." Mike gestures toward a sauntering Roseanne, who has separated herself from Hal and is walking our way. Hal watches her until she arrives, like a date seeing his girl to the door.

I pat the ground next to me and say, "Join us. We need to talk."

She stands unmoving for a moment, studying each of our faces, then sits beside me.

"What about?" Her face is devoid of expression. She knows what this is about, just wants to make us say it.

"You're in pretty deep with Hal, aren't you?" Mike opens the subject.

"I care for him, yes."

"You do know he shot a man," Barbara says. "Is this someone you can trust to not harm you?"

Roseanne bristles. "He said that was an accident. The gun just went off. He's a Christian man, a farmer."

Rachel says, "He was holding it, right?"

"Hal said he was protecting his pigs from being killed by federal agents. He never meant—"

"Oh, God. Stop defending him. You make me sick." Jess rolls onto her side, her back to Roseanne.

"Jess, you don't know—"

Karen interrupts. "Oh, yes, she does, Roseanne."

"At least he tried to stop Mark from raping you."

"That's what he told you?" Jess went from mouth agape to lips pressed tight.

"He wouldn't lie to me." Roseanne shakes her head like a recalcitrant child.

Jess leans in Roseanne's face. "Well, I'm afraid he did. Both he and Bridger cheered Mark on. I was there, so I know what really happened."

That stops Roseanne's defense of Hal in its tracks.

Luci scoots close to Jess and puts her arm around her. At first I think Jess will push her off, but she leans in against Luci and lets her hold her.

I shift to my feet and stir the beans in the heavy silence. "Roseanne, you need to understand it is an us-against-them situation. The lines can't be fuzzy right now. These men are dangerous. All of them. If we figure out some way to stand up to them, we can't have you interfering or discussing our plan with any one of them."

"I understand. You want me to choose." Roseanne stares at her hands in her lap.

"You're damned right," Mike says, her voice raised.

"Well, I'm not a lesbian like the rest of you. When I signed up for this trip, I thought I'd be traveling with ladies."

This brings on raucous laughter.

Roseanne gets to her feet, turns abruptly, and walks head-high to the cook tent.

"So much for that little *tête-à-tête*. Got us nowhere except lines drawn in the sand. Let's eat." I pass out the plates and spoons.

Rachel sits down next to me. "What I can't figure out is why those bastards are hanging around. I'd have thought they would be out of here the first chance they had."

I shift to a more comfortable position. "Maybe they are worn out from hiking over the Continental Divide. My guess is that not one of them has ever walked even to the grocery store."

"Looks like they think they're living in one right now." Rachel pokes the last red coals back to life.

"Perhaps when they've eaten up everything they think of as food, they will go on to greener pastures." Karen leans over to put a stick of wood on the fire.

"Maybe they'll take Roseanne with them," Rachel snorts.

"Don't even think it." But I laugh.

Dusk softens the sharp firs along the horizon. The muffled footfalls of our horses grazing adds to the illusion of peace.

Stormy groans as she pushes herself to her feet. "I'm heading to bed. Long day, and my headache has gotten worse every hour of it."

Barbara looks concerned. "Have you taken anything for it? Come on, I've got something in my tent you can use."

I wish them good night and, one by one, all the women except Rachel head to their bedrolls. Suits me. Funny thing about wilderness. You rarely have time alone, or time for an intimate conversation.

"I'm too tired to sleep," she says.

I throw another stick of wood on the fire to keep the glow high enough to see her face. "So, talk. Tell me how you figured out you're a lesbian." I laugh a little, mostly irony behind it. "Always figure this is an amazing feat for us rural gals, given the general scarcity of people out West as well as the determined heterosexism of the culture. Ha! This interview is not being recorded."

Rachel laughs. "God, what a relief!" Her eyes and mouth turn serious, and she continues. "Other than a girlhood crush, the light came with Margaret."

She pauses so long, I began to wonder if she plans to tell me.

After a quick glance at me, she resumes. "Dr. Margaret Carson came out of the blue and shook up my complacent life. She bought my retiring veterinarian's practice at a time that was crucial to me since I had entered to ride in the hundred-mile-in-one-day Tevis Cup competition. I was wary of a woman vet, I admit, but she won me over. And how."

Rachel mostly looks at the fire as she speaks, and I keep feeding it to stoke her words. "So, where is she now?"

"Close to Boston. Claimed lots of reasons—no cell service was right at the top. Referred to this as barbaric. Hated the wind. And said I was too tough, that I needed to show her my vulnerability. Well, it was too hard for me to do anything other than what I grew up learning I had to do to survive. I think I did change with her. She helped me realize I could ask for help."

"But not quick enough to help your relationship?"

"Actually, it took me a year of crying, raging, and moping around to figure out she would have left eventually, no matter how perfect in her eyes I became."

"Ouch."

"Yeah. Mortifying to realize your lover's access to a cell phone is more important than you. To me, they are somewhat unreliable devices which can be handy when everything works."

"I've found that East-West dynamic to be a conflict, too."

"Your girlfriend leave you?"

I take a few minutes to answer. Full dark has settled around us, sitting in the warm island glow of the flames. The pop of the fire restarts me. "Close to two years ago she, Jane… died. It's a long story, longer than our firewood supply."

"I'm listening."

I laugh a little. "Captive audience, eh?"

Rachel smiles with her eyes and settles into a comfortable position. My voice has a rough start, but eventually my words spin off like sparks through the firelight, into the dark until all the words light a path into my heart.

One long howl cuts the silence. The wild call from a wolf rebounds from the ridges. No sound from the wilderness is as lonely and untamed, except perhaps a loon on a northern lake. Skipper nudges my leg, and I reach a hand to her head. Her growl is more a vibration than a sound. My hackles are erect, too.

A ringing clash comes from the cook tent with a rising thunder of male voices. One hell of an argument is going on inside. With apprehension, we listen to the full-scale dispute;

the background song of the wolf gives the fight an even wilder sound.

The cook tent flap flips open, and Roseanne is propelled out. She turns and looks back, says something we can't hear, then Mark yells, "Stay out of here."

Roseanne stands there a moment, then walks slowly toward our tents. She is sobbing. Rachel squeezes my hand softly, and then she slips into her tent. I pour water over what's left of the fire, making a white cloud of steam and a loud hiss, then duck inside Stormy's tent so I don't have to deal with Roseanne. I feel a flash of sympathy for her, no longer welcome either place.

CHAPTER SEVENTEEN

I'm frying up some green pepper and onions for breakfast and getting ready to pour a pint of Egg Beaters into the mess when I hear a shouted "Halloo."

Bridger comes running to our tents saying urgently, "Get in this tent, everyone. Be quiet. Someone's coming."

He shoves Sue toward the tent, and she stumbles and falls. Her glasses come off, and Bridger steps on them in the scuffle. I hear a sickening crunch.

"My glasses," Sue wails.

"Quiet!" Bridger hisses and pushes her through the tent flap.

I look over my shoulder to see what has the men freaked and get a quick glimpse of four people loaded with tall backpacks approaching from the river.

Bridger kneels by the fire as though he's the one cooking. I stand at the crack in the closed flap to see what's happening. Bridger snarls over his shoulder. "Don't show any part of you, or there will be fucking hell to pay."

I stay there and continue watching trying to hear what's being said. Behind me, Sue is bemoaning her broken glasses. "I can't see without them. Everything's a blur."

Mark has approached the backpackers: two Native American men with long black hair in ponytails; a white man and woman, kind of hippie-like. I see one of the Indian guys motion toward the pass, then at the camp. I can't hear anything he says, but Mark's voice carries. "You can't stay here. I've got a bunch of dudes I'm outfitting."

The backpackers look around, some more unintelligible speech floats my way. They look toward us and Bridger lifts his hand in a guy greeting.

"All out on a ride." Mark waves up toward where he's seen us drive the horses. "Needle Falls. They'll all be back soon. You'll have to camp farther up the trail."

I notice Hal is not in sight. Too identifiable.

The tall Indian guy laughs, shakes his head, and I just manage to hear, "We planned on camping here."

"Plan again," Mark says with a growl.

The backpackers lose their smiles, turn, and move on up the path. Animated talk between them is lost on the wind, but they are pissed.

Karen whispers a question, and I turn to her and say, "With any luck, they'll talk to the right person. That kind of rudeness doesn't happen often, especially from outfitters. In the backcountry people are always welcome to join an existing camp. They'll know something's not right."

"Any real chance a ranger could come?"

"Don't get your hopes up. They've got a two-day hike before they even have a snowball's chance in hell of meeting up with anyone. And they could be hiking north along the wall at the base of the cliff."

I open the tent flap to find Bridger gone and the onions burning.

I try to salvage breakfast with the buzz of the women's voices behind me. Sue recovers her glasses from the dirt. She tenderly tries to straighten them out, but they are beyond salvage.

Mike says, "Maybe we can fix them, honey." She puts her arm around her partner.

Sue's face looks naked, tears streaming down her cheeks. She tenderly places the parts in her shirt pocket as though they will do her some good eventually.

Everyone else is speculating about the backpackers. "Will they bring someone back to save us? Alert the authorities? Helicopter in with machine guns?" The speculation is endless.

I finally say, "We've got to stay centered. No one is going to save us. We have to get ourselves out of this mess. So, eat."

I roll up scrambled eggs inside tortillas and hand them out. If anything, the appearance of the backpackers has depressed me. They are free, we aren't. Between the food and my outburst, the women gather silently around the fire.

Finally someone speaks. Kamau says, "The outhouse stinks."

A few murmured yeahs agree. I stand up. "At least I can do something about that." I go to the five-gallon aluminum trash can sitting behind the outhouse, scoop up a generous amount of lime, and dump it down the hole. A swarm of flies lifts up to buzz around the inside of the pole outhouse. I can't imagine what the men's outhouse on the other side of the cook tent is like. Nor do I want to.

Rachel comes up to me. "How about we fight this waiting for the men to make up their minds with our fly rods?"

I brighten considerably. "You're on!"

While we're gathering our gear, Sue sees us. She says, "You mean to tell me you're just going off to fish?"

We both stop what we're doing and look at her. Rachel says, "Well, yeah."

"Got any better ideas?" I ask her.

"How can you just go off and have fun, at a time like this?"

Rachel smiles so all her teeth show. "Personally, I can't think of a better time. What else are we supposed to do, sit around wringing our hands?"

I duck my head so my shit-eating grin isn't so obvious.

Rachel and I walk off past the corrals, chatting about fly-fishing gear.

Mark shouts, "Hey! Where do you think you're going?"

"Stuff it," Rachel breathes.

I shout back, "Fishing."

"We get the fish," he yells.

I turn and just stare at him. "What is this? You think you get everything? What are we, your mothers? Your wives? If you want fish, go catch them."

I join back with Rachel, and we walk on down the edge of the river. On either side of the rushing water round river rock border islands of persistent alders in straggling clumps, survivors of the spring run-off flooding. I've caught some nice rainbows in a deep pool just up ahead.

We drop our kit bags, dig out fly boxes, and stand head-to-head discussing which fly to use. "There's always grasshoppers," she says, fingering the rubber-legged look-alikes.

"Why don't you try those? I might go for the Royal Wullfs." I tie one on the end of my tippet, put the fly box away, shouldering the bag, and I move down river to the edge of the hole. A windblown snag rests on the bank, its top hanging down into the water, and if I were a fish, that's where I'd be.

I cast my neon green line up current of the snag and let the fly float down past the submerged part. The fly travels serenely above the dark shadows and then disappears, pulled down by a hungry fish. I set the hook and take up the line. The tip of the rod bends as I fight the fish on the end. The fish is going back to the shelter of the snag and suddenly there's no tension, my rod snaps back to straight, and I'm drawing in an empty line. Took my Royal Wulff, too.

Up river, Rachel is having more luck. Her rod is bending out over the water, and a fish breaks. I see her scoop up a nice rainbow with her net. Her face is radiant.

I tie on another fly, an elk hair caddis, and give the water around the snag a second go. There's a strike. Not much fight though. I reel in the line to see a small rainbow on the end, flashing silver in the sun. So small it will get its freedom to grow into a bigger fish.

Out of the dark depths of the pool, a monster fish rises, opens its mouth, and takes my tiny rainbow. The thing seems to look me in the eye as it swallows the fish; the line breaks from its sheer weight as it sinks back to the dark.

"Jeezus! What was that?" Rachel leans at the waist, trying to see into the water.

"Bull trout."

"My God! That must be three feet long. Bulls are legend on my side of the Rockies."

"I'm glad they're catch and release only."

"Well, that one released itself."

I laugh. "Sure did. I've only got a ten pound test line."

I re-rig my line with a new leader and fly, and we pull three more good-sized rainbow out of the water, then move down to the next pool where we each catch eating size fish.

"Guess we need to head back." I take out my pocketknife, kneel by the water, and clean the fish, letting everything slide into the water. Any scent from the fish will be erased.

Rachel draws in a long, deep breath. She turns slowly, looking at this wild place. "Funny, isn't it? I live on a ranch most people would consider remote, but I never seem to get enough of the wild."

I smile at her as I cut a thin willow branch to hold the fish through the gills. "You'd think we ranch gals would head for the nearest city, but I'm the same way. Most often, I aim for something even wilder than where I live."

"The solitude and peace of open spaces, room for your shoulders, and a good horse under you doesn't hurt."

"Not at all." Our smiles hold, joining our gaze, her brown eyes with my gray. I could tell we had similar history and just plain liked each other.

Rachel's focus changes to the powerful river chuckling over the big rocks on its way to the Pacific. "Damn. The fishing's good here. It is a treat to be away from that nightmare, even for a short while."

"Almost forget that we're living as hostages, eh? I think things may change soon. Those backpackers have reminded them that they need to get going, that other people could show up. In the meantime, we can cook these up for lunch with a side of rice. With any luck, we can come back."

"You mean if the men clear out." Rachel breaks her four-piece Winston rod down and slides it back in the tube. I thought my Orvis a nice one until I saw hers, light and balanced. Maybe I'll drive down to Sheridan and pick up one of Winston's bamboo rods. Never could even dream of dropping near a thousand dollars on my own amusement before Jane's death.

We walk slowly back to camp, comparing the pros and cons of various fly rods.

CHAPTER EIGHTEEN

The glare we get from Mark when we walk back into camp is priceless. We have eight fat fish on a willow branch, and I'm hoping the aroma of fresh fried fish will permeate the entire valley.

We get enthusiastic greetings at our camp. The only one not ecstatic to see us and our fish is Kamau. Mike comes up to me with a grin the size of Kansas on her face. "Wow! Those are big fish."

Rachel says, "Well, you should see the one that got away." She sets to cooking some rice.

Mike lifts her head and laughs. "Oh, yeah."

"No kidding. There is a fish in that river that would scare you if you were swimming."

"Oh, go on." Mike has a half-smile on her face. She directs her gaze at me, hoping I'll dispel the fish story.

"There are some big ones in there."

Rachel says, "I could see these moving shadows in the deep part, like sharks lurking. At least three feet long."

I hide my smile, kneeling down to mix up a batter for the fish. I whisk up corn meal, some Egg Beaters, and pepper, dip in the fish, and toss a bit of water into the skillet to see if the peanut oil is hot. The water dances. The aroma of frying fish calls to our carnivorous origins.

I see Karen has a pot of beans next to the rice Rachel started. We can eat the beans for dinner. When the trout are cooked, I split each fish down the spine, open it up, and lift out the intact bone with all the hairy ribs. I drop the bones into the fire. As each plate gets presented in front of me, I gingerly lift the tender steaming white flesh, add a scoop of rice, and say you're welcome.

Everyone's been served, and there's still half a fish resting in the pan. I ask Kamau, "You sure you don't want any?"

She makes a gagging sound. "I take that for a no." I split the half again and give Rachel half of Kamau's share, and I wolf down the other.

"No need to be rude, Kamau," Luci scolds. She wipes her mouth daintily on her sleeve cuff.

Stormy says, "Can't tell you how good that was. I'll do all your chores, trade my body's pleasures, anything for more."

"In that case, I'll send my fly into the water morning, noon, and night."

The devil looks up at me through her eyelashes, slips the tip of her tongue around the edge of her upper lip, and groans.

I blush like a madwoman. My eyes flash sideways at Rachel. Everyone sitting around in the fish afterglow laughs. "How could you turn that down?" Barbara asks.

Rachel says, "Hey, perhaps I can trade fish for sexual favors." She looks around. "No takers? I'm disappointed."

I see a little wiggle to one side, and Candace's hand comes halfway up. The other hides the smile on her face.

"Oh, here! You've got a taker," Barbara says, pointing to Candace.

I'm sitting with my back against a tree, legs straight out and my dish resting in my lap when Mark and Bridger approach. Hal isn't with them, and Roseanne never came back to the tent last night.

My mood has been seriously improved with the first pure protein in days. Some of my contentment comes from the fact that those guys didn't get a share. I flip my tin dish into the basin at my feet, say, "What's up, boys?"

Karen and Stormy rise to their feet, and Jess heads for the inside of our tent.

Mark says, "We decided we'll take three horses and one packhorse and leave tomorrow, at dawn."

"A packhorse will just give you problems," I state.

"You just don't want us to take the grub." Mark smiles knowingly.

"Do any of you know how to pack an animal so the weighted sides of the panniers are even or lead a loaded packhorse on a narrow trail, or what can happen when the lead rope from the packhorse runs under your horse's tail? You might arrive where you want to stop that first night, but you won't have a clue as to how to unload it or load up again the next day. If you want to get where you're going, just pack the saddlebags and tie your bedrolls on the back of the saddles."

Mark and Bridger eye each other and Mark nods his head to the right. They step off a short distance for a whispered conference. Simultaneously, they turn back to face the women. "Okay. Three riding horses, good ones now."

I glance at the sky, judging how much daylight is left to round the horses up. "Didn't give us much notice."

Mark's voice is cold. "Just bring them in."

"You'll have to show us how to put the gear on the horses," Bridger adds.

I glance at Stormy. "We better get a move on."

Jess is standing just inside the tent flap, and I go over to her to get descriptions of the horses to bring back. "Just bring them all. I'll pick out the ones to use when they're here."

I catch up Buck and arrive at the tie-up bar at the same time as Stormy and her bay horse.

Relief surges through my body. Soon we will be free of this nightmare.

Skipper follows us to the hitch rail to watch what we're going to do. She knows whenever I have a horse on a lead, I'm going someplace. She barks one excited bark as we mount up. "Come on, girl."

We trot where we can to make time riding toward Gladiator. They aren't in the big meadow where we left them. We ride a little farther. The tinkle of the lead mare's bell comes from a small meadow on the far side of a tongue of firs. We soon spot the grazing horses, and I dismount, pull Buck's bridle, and hang it on the saddle horn. I buckle on the hobbles and look up to see Stormy with a quizzical expression on her face.

"What're you doing?" Stormy rides up to me.

"Get off your horse, girl. I want you."

Understanding floods her face, and she jumps off her bay, taking off the mare's bridle and hobbling her up.

Our bodies meet like starving wolves, devouring the time apart. We sink to the ground, horses politely grazing around us, while we unzip, unbutton, desperate to get to the skin, the warm flesh. My lips nuzzle into her sweet-smelling hair, nip her ears, slide my tongue down her neck, back up into the hollow behind her ear. My breath comes in short pants. Stormy's hands grip my shoulders as my mouth ranges the round of her belly. Her sounds echo the birdcalls from the junipers.

It all happens too fast after wanting her for so long.

Tincture of bruised grass reaches my nostrils as I lie there staring up at the sky. She rolls across the carpet of bright wildflowers into my arms and purrs. I touch her face, and she turns to me like a sunflower. Her long fingers reach out to a blue harebell, plucking it from its neighbors. With a playful light in her eyes, she runs the flower down the edge of my cheek from ear to chin. I laugh and kiss her fingers as they pass by.

The sun gilds Gladiator from the west. I sit up slowly to slide into my shirt, the nearest piece of clothing. We turn to each other, imprinting the moment. "Too long," I observe.

Stormy sighs. "We're using up the daylight."

"In a good way. Those boys have no idea how long rounding up the horses takes." I catch up Buck and put her bridle on. Skip has probably been watching us the whole time. "You get an eyeful?" I say to her, and she wags her tail.

"Go bring 'em in." The dog jumps to her feet and is a flash of gray and white, streaking in a wide half-circle behind the herd. She barks once and zooms back and forth, getting them moving, driving them toward us.

Stormy leads off with the bell mare, and I wait for the last horse. Skip catches up with me in the fading light, her flat pink tongue hanging out and pleasure in her eyes to be doing the work she was meant to.

The horses remember the grain pellets and don't need any urging. We charge across the rushing White River in the dusk, splashing water over the horses' shoulders, and then we gallop toward the corrals. The gate is standing open and I ride up and close it when they've all entered. The horses circle with some bucks and kicks, and then they settle into being tame again. Stormy and I tie our horses to the rail, and I get a half bag of grain to reward the stock. Not much, but hopefully a bite each.

I say to Stormy, "Go ahead and get some chow. I'll finish with the horses."

Karen comes out to help us. "I think it's going to work," she whispers in my ear.

"Have you worked out with Jess which horses to let them have?"

"I think Jess is making the selection." I feel her start beside me in the dark.

"Took you long enough." Bridger appears in the beam of Karen's flashlight.

"Scattered all over the mountain. They're fat and happy." I take the saddle off my mare and sling it over the rail.

"Nice saddle," Bridger observes.

I grunt. "Saddles fit the horse. We'll pick out the ones that fit your horses."

"I want this one." Bridger strokes the basket weave tooling on the skirt.

I stop what I'm doing and stare at him. "Well, get over it. I made this saddle—"

"No way! You didn't make this saddle."

I ignore him and toss a canvas manty over both saddles and lash it down for the night. No way is he going to ride off on the saddle I made. It fits both me and my horse like a well-tailored suit.

"Every thing's a jumble, piled up the way you have it in the tent. Take us a while to sort it out in the morning."

"You're a bossy bitch." Bridger puffs himself up. "Better watch yourself."

"Let's go eat." Karen touches my arm and we walk away. "You'll be excited. Beans again tonight."

Her gentle Buddhist being knows how to defuse me and how to come to harmonious ends. I admire her. Could use a little more of that patience. Is it some sort of lesson for me to have loved a Quaker and be in this mess with a Buddhist? My suspicions are that I could use some of both teachings.

At the flap of Karen's tent, she says to me, "Let's meet again in our tent."

"Yes. We need to figure some things out."

Rachel hands me a bowl of hot beans and rice, and I squat by the glow of the fire to eat.

Afterward, I lie down on my sleeping bag. Skipper curls up under my arm, and I let myself drift back to the scent of grass and Stormy on my fingers. I lift them to my nose. Yes, she's still there. I lick my fingertips to further imprint her on my brain. Luci and Kamau are in the tent with me and before long Luci says, "Let's go."

I heave myself to my feet and tell Skip to wait here.

CHAPTER NINETEEN

Once we are all gathered, Karen says, "Now that there is the prospect of the men leaving us, we have some decisions to make. First thing to deal with is getting Jess out of here to a doctor. The second is that today is the twelfth, and we have four more days before we are due out. Are you up for taking back our camp, changing the energy, and spending the rest of the time here, or do you just want to get back to civilization along with Jess?"

The women mull this over.

"I haven't seen the Chinese Wall yet." Stormy breaks the silence.

Rachel says, "The fishing's good, and I'd like to see the view from the top of that wall. And you know, odd as this sounds, I love being with all of you women."

Candace slips her arm around Rachel's waist and tilts her head against her. "Really. There is that."

Rachel smiles and gives her a squeeze.

Barbara says, "I'd like to run up to Needle Falls."

Luci looks at her like she's crazy. "Alone? Why ever for?"

"Have to keep in shape." Barbara half smiles. "I run marathons around the Seattle area." She holds up one hand, fingers up, palm out. "Oh, I never win, except I'm getting to the age that I'll soon be earning 'oldest runner' awards."

Awed laughter greets this piece of information. "I hope I'm getting around as well as you when I have white hair," Luci says.

Karen points to her white hair and smiles. "Just keep doing what you love."

Candace says, "Other than dressage, what I love is a box of chocolates."

Roseanne is quiet, and I wonder if she is thinking about her new love riding away tomorrow.

Mike says, "I came on this trip to see the Chinese Wall. Can't we take a day and do that?"

"I don't see why not," Karen says. "What about the rest of you?"

Barbara, Luci, Candace, and Kamau all agree that the wall was their goal and damned if the men would cheat them of this experience. Roseanne is noticeably silent.

"There's another ride you might want to take. Gladiator is very impressive. That's up the way we run the horses. It's good for a short day's ride with beautiful rock formations." I look around at the women who need to have some escape to this madness we've encountered. "The day after we've seen the wall we can ride up that way, then take a day off." I glance at Rachel. "Catch some more fish."

"I'd like to learn something about fly fishing," Barbara says.

"Come with us. I'll teach you." Rachel sends Barbara a warm smile, and I wonder if something's brewing there. I feel a strange stab of jealousy course through me, and I then have to wonder, *where did that come from?*

"With the men gone, we'll have more access to the river," I observe.

Candace says, "Those men are such scabs. I will be so happy to see their backsides."

"Now, Candace, all men aren't bad." Sue leans up against Mike with her hand resting on her spouse's arm.

"Don't give me that bullshit. Honestly, my experience proves otherwise."

Karen is looking thoughtful, and I know she's about to come out with some we-are-all-like-ants thing.

But Sue beats her to it. "There are good men in the world. Mike is going to prove that point."

"What?" Candace, Stormy, and I all say it at the same time with varying degrees of incredulity.

Mike's face is near as red as my Pendleton jacket back home. Her voice begins so low we all say "What?" again.

"I'm transitioning." She makes a gagging, throat-clearing sound. "You know…some day I'll be a man."

"Oh. My. God. Well, Fuck me!" Candace says. She is staring at Mike as though she had metamorphosed into a slug. Her lip curls into a snarl. "Why on God's green earth would you want to do that?"

Barbara puts her hand on Candace's shoulder. "Perhaps you need to be more understanding. This is never an easy decision for anyone to make."

Kamau frowns. "What are you, Candace, coming out of the dark ages? Gender is what you want it to be. Just because we came out of the womb one way doesn't mean that's fixed for life."

Mike is intensely uncomfortable, looking back and forth from Candace to Barbara to Kamau.

"Then why did he she want to come on an all-women trip? Bizarre." Candace makes a retching sound and turns her back on Mike. "Makes me feel creepy, like there's a male infiltrator in our midst."

We all seem to be unable to keep ourselves from glancing at Roseanne.

Barbara steps impatiently forward. "I've just about heard enough, Candace. Get over it."

Candace puts her knuckles on her hips, "Well? I didn't come on this trip to be with a quasi man."

"Ouch," Mike says.

Kamau groans. "I don't believe this dialogue."

I figure it is time to say something. "None of us planned to be hostages, under the control of three renegade men, either." I take a long look at Candace, who seems to be having the hardest time with the trans information. "Most of us have a knot in our rope."

"What's that supposed to mean?" Candace turns on me like a spitting cat.

"Work it out."

Karen smoothly segues us back to the original conversation. "You know our reservations at the bed and breakfast aren't until the scheduled end of our trip." Karen takes a breath. "So, it is agreed we will stay our full number of days, one to take back our camp and one for a ride up to the Wall?"

"And perhaps time for more fly fishing?" It is, of course, Rachel. I smile at her in agreement.

Luci rubs her stomach. "I'll be here with skillet at the ready."

"Okay," Karen says, "So, back to Jess."

Jess murmurs some mild resistance to anything special for her.

"Who will ride out with Jess?" Karen glances around at the group.

Sue holds up her hand. "I won't be able to see a thing. I'll ride back with you, Jess."

A sigh like a soft breeze of relief comes from the women.

"Good," I say firmly. "As soon as those guys leave in the

morning, we'll saddle two horses and you can head out. While we are getting things together, Karen, could you make them some food to take with them?"

Karen nods and holds up the keys to the van. "Do you want these?"

"No. I'll unhitch my gooseneck and take the truck. When we get to Augusta, I'll go to the sheriff's and alert them that those guys will be coming out of the White River drainage." Jess turns to Sue. "Thanks for offering to come with me. It will be a hard ride, faster than when we came in. Sure you're up for it?"

"Yes. I think someone needs to go with you. I won't be much use as a lookout, but maybe I'll be company."

We agree once we get the men out, we will take a day to recoup, straighten the place up, and reclaim our space. The following day, we'll all ride up to the Wall.

Most of the women have left for their sleeping bags when Karen asks Jess, "Do you mind coming out with Miles and me in the morning to saddle the horses and get those men on their way?"

Jess smiles, and it's one that looks cunning. "Sure thing. I want to be there."

"You're not up to something, are you, Jess?" I worry she is going to have her revenge at our expense.

"Oh, they're good horses. Just have a few quirks."

Later that night a rustle brings me to full alert. I get a glimpse of Roseanne sneaking out of the tent.

I go over our conversation and can't think of anything that would harm us for those three men to know. Nothing better mess up the great departure. I am so over their hubristic, testosterone-ridden, slovenly ways.

CHAPTER TWENTY

Stormy, Jess, and I get up before dawn. Roseanne is not in her sleeping bag. No movement or light comes from the cook tent. Stormy and I catch our horses, remove the hobbles, and tie the mares up at far end of the rail.

"Jess," I call softly to her. "You want to tell us which five to sort out so we only have to feed them? Later we'll drive all the rest back up to grass."

"I think that one Sue rode in on is a good one for her, and my sorrel quarter horse gelding." We catch them and lead them into a side corral.

"Then for the men, that one with the four white socks." Jess points to a small gelding.

Stormy gets a halter on the unwilling beast after walking him down. "And that one with the bald face."

I know this horse to have a chronic limp. I say as much to Jess.

"They won't notice." She smiles slightly.

The third one she selects is a good-looking black mare. I comment on the horse's quality and Jess replies, "Good looker, but will buck on occasion."

"I see you've put some thought into this. What's wrong with the gelding with stockings?"

"Will bite the bejeezus out of you if you aren't watching. He's normally in the pack string."

"Works for me." I smile at her, the first genuine smile between us.

The mare and two geldings are tied up at the rail. Jess and Sue's horses are in a small side corral where they can eat in peace. Jess says, "Let me deal with the biter. He knows me and won't try anything."

We hang feed buckets in front of the men's mounts, with about two pounds each of pellets, brush them down, and are ready to gather saddles when Mark comes out of the tent with a mug of coffee in his hand. That was one of the things I missed like crazy, but they weren't giving any of it over.

I yell, "Time to fetch the saddles. Are your saddlebags packed?"

Mark tosses his coffee dregs to one side, then silently turns and goes back into the tent.

"Come on, Jess. Let's get the saddles."

Jess stands unmoving. "I'm not going back in there."

"Okay. Let's go back to our tent and get a couple of other women. Can you describe the saddles that go with these animals?"

"The slick fork with bell stirrups, that old roping saddle with a floral pattern, and a rough out saddle with a Mexican horn. If you can get them to the rail, I'll make sure we match them up to the horses."

Rachel and Mike offer to come with me. When we get to the cook tent, I busy myself finding the right saddles in all the jumble of tack. Roseanne is there.

Hal leans toward her, whispering. She says to Hal, "Take me with you."

Hal's jaw drops. "Oh, baby...I..."

"In a pig's ass she's coming with us. What the fuck have

you been up to, Hal?" Mark slams down his mug, coffee shooting straight up.

I feel like asking the same question. I get one of the saddles, show Rachel the other, kick the Mexican saddle to indicate which one to Mike, and get out of there. Halfway back to the corrals, I double up with laughter. Stormy comes up to me and asks, "What's so funny?"

I can't talk, but Rachel can. "Roseanne is in there making a fool of herself. She is pleading with Hal to take her with them."

Stormy's jaw drops. "You're not kidding?"

When I get myself under control, I say, "Here take this. I've got to get bridles and saddle pads." I return, cautiously opening the tent flap. Roseanne is pleading, wringing her hands. Both Bridger and Mark are raging at Hal. I get the bridles and pads I need and head back out of there.

While we bridle the horses, I tell the others about Roseanne's bid for love.

"It's so sad," Stormy says.

"Sad? It's pathetic."

"Miles, I'm surprised at you. I thought you'd be more compassionate."

Her criticism stings.

I say to her, "Well, let's get our horses saddled so we can run the rest of the stock back up the valley when we're ready." I try not to remember the tenderness we felt for each other yesterday up that very valley.

Jess oversees our sorting out, walking back and forth on the fringe of the action, ready to bolt. She says, "Leave the black so Miles can show Mark how to saddle. Charlene, you saddle the bald face, and I'll get the biter. One of us should hold his head while the guy mounts. Bridger or Hal, doesn't

matter. Then I'm going back to the tent to pack up my stuff."
Jess is the only one who calls Stormy by her original name.

The men are taking their time getting ready. We stand
together, listening to them argue. A sliver of yellow off to the
east shows the sun is making an effort to rise above White
River Pass. Half-light brings things into fuzzy focus.

The wolf is back. Hard to tell where the echoing howl
originates. The women draw closer to me. Rachel says, "God,
how wild the sound."

Karen stares toward the dark mass of mountains. "All my
life I've wanted this."

Jess says, "We hear them in Yellowstone. Buggers are
everywhere since they were reintroduced."

"They've always been here. One of the last holdout
places." My ears scan the mountains like radar antenna, trying
to pinpoint the sound.

Jess shifts her feet. "Let's get this show on the road."

I approach the tent and call out, "All set. Mark, why don't
I show you how to saddle a horse?"

"I know how," is his grumpy reply.

"Then, the other guys. They might need to know."

The three men leave the tent carrying their saddlebags and
bedrolls. They come to a sudden halt when they hear the call
of the wolf. Mark reaches for his pistol.

"What's that? Coyotes?" Hal cocks his head.

"Hell, no." A big smile crosses Bridger's face. "I never…"

"They better stay back." Mark cocks the gun, aims in the
general direction of the sound, and fires.

Everyone jumps at the sound, then holds still and listens.
All is silent.

Mark shoves the gun back in the holster. "Better take that
as a warning."

Stormy says, "Put your saddlebags over the rail here and we'll lace them on the back once we figure out who's riding what."

Bridger keeps his saddlebags over his shoulder.

Stormy pats the rail. "You can put them here."

He jerks back a step. "Don't touch my bags."

Roseanne is still tugging at Hal's sleeve. He pats her, tucks a piece of paper in his jeans, and promises to write. She's crying now. I roll my eyes and hold the biter for Hal, who tears himself away from Roseanne and blows her a kiss. *Oh, my God!*

I keep one eye on Mark's inept saddling procedure. He slings the saddle, slamming it against the horse's side. The mare jumps away. Mark jerks the lead and says, "Damn you! Stand still."

Mark tries again and manages to get the saddle on, shoving it forward. From here I can see the pad's rucked up and only halfway under the saddle.

Meanwhile Stormy helps Bridger mount. Once he's in the saddle, he says, "Hey! I thought I told you I wanted that other saddle. Get that one and switch them."

I ignore him and go to Mark's side. "You've got the idea, but make sure the saddle pad is smooth and sitting up a little further." I take the saddle all the way off and show him how the pad must be. "If there are wrinkles, it will sore the horse's back." I easily lift the saddle back into place, slide it back a hair, and settle it, doing up the cinch.

"Here, I know how to do that." Mark takes over, slamming his knee into the mare's side. She puts her ears back and raises her head, cow kicking with one hind leg. Her hoof grazes his knee, and he jumps back swearing.

"You don't have to do that. Kneeing a horse doesn't make them let the air out. I know a lot of people think that, but all you do is piss them off." I show him you can slide the latigo up one notch at a time. "Walk her around a minute, then take it up one more notch."

Rising euphoria at the thought of their departure makes me giddy. Tightening my lips, I suppress a laugh.

Meanwhile, Bridger is grousing about wanting my saddle. "You cheated me out of it," he claims.

"Oh, shut up, Bridger," Mark says once he's in the saddle.

He kicks his horse, which shoots out from under him, landing him on his backside in the dirt. Stunned, he lies there a moment, then stands, mad as hell. "I thought you said these horses are gentle!"

"They are. Just don't kick them. All you need to do is close your leg on her side." I am struggling to keep my face devoid of the pleasure I'm experiencing to see him land on his butt. I imagine Jess is in the shadows watching with high amusement.

Marks hands are shaking when he grabs the horn and the cantle to help him mount. He is breathing short quick breaths when he turns to me and says, "Hold him. Tight!" Mark manages to mount again. "Okay. Let's ride!"

I say, "Write when you find work."

Hal's stirrups are a little long, and he's fishing around for them, lurching around in the saddle. Bridger slaps his horse on the neck with his reins, probably like he's seen done in cowboy movies. I figure if they make it across the river still on top of their mounts, it will be a miracle. I pray that is so.

Roseanne's face is devastated as she watches them disappear through the trees. A strange sound comes out of her, something between a wail and a moan.

Listening to the splashes, I guess they've all made it across and sigh with relief. Echoing sighs come from Rachel and Stormy.

As soon as they're on their way down the trail, I get the saddles Jess told me to get earlier. We have their horses saddled by the time Sue and Jess leave the tents and walk toward us. Karen hands them two packages of food. "Godspeed," she whispers. As we watch them ride away we all move closer to each other, except Roseanne, who runs, stumbling, to the tent.

CHAPTER TWENTY-ONE

Mark plunges into the river first, the black mare carefully setting her feet on the large rocks. Bridger and Hal's geldings follow.

Bridger grips the large flat Mexican saddle horn with both hands and draws his feet up to avoid the splashing water. "Shit, man, can you imagine what this would have been like on foot?"

"So, Bridger, you might have gotten a little wet?" Mark laughs.

"More than wet, we would have been swept away." Bridger's horse lurches up the far bank, and the man grabs leather for dear life.

The biter is slow and cautious, balancing Hal on his back. He places his hooves with great care crossing the water.

Mark manages to turn his horse left to follow the trail downstream. Hal and Bridger's horses mill around, bumping into each other, confused about where to go. Bridger pulls his rein hand out to one side to direct his horse, but since he doesn't release it soon enough, he just goes in a circle.

Mark yells back over his shoulder, "Get those horses straightened out! We don't have all day."

The horses are reluctant to head in a direction unfamiliar

to them, but eventually Hal and Bridger get them to follow Mark's black mare.

The path leads along the river, pine needles muffling the sound of the hooves. All three horses settle into a steady walk. The sun breaks free of the Rocky Mountain Front, highlighting the smooth, waxy gray bark of the aspens. Small eddies of wind stir the trembling leaves. The river sparkles over the rocks, bright water rushing to the Pacific Ocean.

"Hey, this isn't so hard," Hal yells. "This is a great little horse."

"This is the life," Bridger says, his horse swinging along at a walk. "I used to dream about doing this, riding a horse along a mountain trail. Riding is easy."

"Just don't fall off," Mark yells over his shoulder. "I'm not going to get you back on."

"You should have made that dyke give me her saddle, Mark. Why didn't you?"

"Oh, will you shut up about that saddle? You've got one, don't you?"

After about an hour, Hal says, "How much farther, Mark?"

"Hell. I don't know, why?"

"I'm a little sore. This saddle is rubbing my balls off. Let's stop and eat a burrito and rest our butts for a minute."

Mark reluctantly agrees, and the three men get off their horses. "This will take forever at this rate."

Hal hands out the burritos he'd made first thing that morning with canned beans and the last of the cheese. Midway through chewing the first mouthful, his horse's head snakes around, teeth flashing, and the gelding grabs Hal's arm in a painful, vise-like grip. Hal screams and drops his burrito, slapping the horse hard on the neck. "You miserable piece of shit," he yells, red-faced.

He bends over with one eye on the animal and picks up his

burrito. He wipes fir needles from the end and takes another mouthful.

Meanwhile, Bridger and Mark are laughing their fool heads off.

"Not as comfy off the horse, I guess," Mark says.

"Guess they gave you the pick of the litter." Bridger smirks.

"Come on. We want to get to that ranger's place and the canoe tonight. We can spend the night there and get rid of these horses in the morning."

"Not too soon." Hal narrows his eyes at the horse's ears, laid flat.

"What if the ranger is there?" Bridger says, shoving half his burrito into his saddlebag.

"We'll take care of him." Mark shoves his foot in the stirrup, jamming the horse with his toe. The mare jumps forward, then spins to face Mark, once again on his back in the dirt. "This is getting old."

Barely suppressed giggles bring Mark to his feet in a rage. "Not funny!"

Bridger nonchalantly sticks his foot in the stirrup and swings up, kicking his horse on the rump as his leg crosses over behind the saddle. He isn't quite in the saddle when the horse steps forward, but manages to cling on and not wind up in the dirt like Mark. He sits up straight to Mark's uproarious laughter.

"Don't go overboard. Wasn't that funny." Bridger sneers.

The men ride in silence for a while with Mark in the lead. Hal squirms in the saddle. "How much farther?" he calls ahead. "My ass is killing me, and I've got to pee."

"Get over it," Mark shoots back without turning. "You are such a whiner."

The river is close on their left, sparkling in the sunlight.

Nearing some dense alders and willows, Mark's horse comes to an abrupt halt. "Get on, you dumb animal!" He kicks the horse. She ignores him, her ears sharply pointed at the alder thicket.

The bushes crackle as a creature roars, and Mark is suddenly staring at eye level face-to-face with a large grizzly reared up on his hind feet. The bear roars, mouth wide open, his teeth glinting behind the red snarl. Mark can smell the bear's rank breath. His mare spins, the bear slaps her hindquarters, and she kicks out, with a mighty jump forward. Mark claws at any part of the saddle that will keep him on but knows he's falling. He lands under the front legs of the grizzly.

The black mare rams into Bridger's horse, head up, nostrils red and round, then shoots past Hal, his face contorted in fear. Hal only has a brief view of the grizzly on top of Mark before his horse spins to join the other two horses galloping back up the trail. He desperately hangs on to anything he can lay a hand on, but he is all over the saddle and he has lost his stirrups.

Mark's screams echo up the narrow valley, following the horsemen until they abruptly end in silence.

The horses run on top of each other, clustering together, bumping and scraping saddles and packs, hot on the heels of Mark's horse. Four long, bleeding gashes like Indian pony war paint decorate the black's hindquarters, the smell of blood heightening their fear.

The trail is not wide enough to handle the panic-driven horses, heads held high, ears flicking back, foam flying from their mouths. Bridger leans forward like a jockey, hands gripping the saddle's breastplate straps. Hal is leaning back, gripping the saddle horn, his unwieldy body trying to balance the horse's erratic movements. The horse comes too close to a tree, and Hal's knee rams into it. He feels a searing pain.

No longer able to grip with his legs, he falls, landing on some rocks. All breath is pushed from him, and he works his chest trying to pull air into his lungs. His lips form Bridger's name. The sound of Bridger's horse galloping on the narrow trail fades to a terrible hush.

Hal gasps for breath and curls up, praying the grizzly is far enough back it won't come for him, too. Having needed to pee, his bladder lets go now, flooding the insides of both legs with warmth. He is finally able to breathe again and uses his breath for prayer. "God, help me. Oh God, what have I done that was so horrible?" Sickness floods him like the urine. "I killed a man. This is your way of punishing me."

Hal curls up in a fetal position, his guts tight with terror.

He huddles against a rock, listening for any sound back down the trail.

CHAPTER TWENTY-TWO

I hold up the gun and holster I retrieved from the feed rack. "Guess I'll need to make a new rig." Tooth marks fray the leather down to the metal of the gun.

"Good thing one of the horses didn't set it off. Battle at the OK Corral." Stormy smiles; a dimple forms in her left cheek.

Kamau touches the purple-black metal of the gun. "They carry so much more power than just the bullets, don't they?"

I nod and wrap the belt around the holster. "Depends on who's holding them."

The day is heavy, humid. But the atmosphere is light, laughter and chatter filling the air. It is so good to hear everyone joking and speaking normally, hard at work making our camp ours again.

The pack and riding saddles are all neatly stored on the rail again, with canvas manties protecting them from any weather. Right after Jess and Sue rode away, Stormy and I drove the remaining horses out to graze.

The men have been gone for only a couple of hours, and it's already so hot I'm sweating. I wipe my forehead with my bandanna and return to the cook tent. The women are all reclaiming it, except Roseanne, who sits just outside on one of the white plastic chairs. Her face is dark, eyebrows lowered, and she's hunched over.

"Want to read?" I ask her. "I've got a Carsen Taite novel in my kit."

"I don't know why this happens to me. I know he's gone and never coming back. I can't think about anything but the fact I'll never see him again."

"And you'd be better off if you don't. You know what pisses me off, Roseanne?" She turns her dark gaze up at me. "It's that Hal so completely convinced you he is a wonderful person."

"Nobody good has ever loved me. I thought if he prayed, he was a good person, don't you see? Since his wife died three years ago, he has been in deep mourning." Her voice rose in a thin whine. "But then when I realized that he lied to me…it took me until just now to believe Jess." In a softer voice, she added, "There is no reason for her to lie."

I take a deep breath. "Don't let him have so much of who you are."

"Who am I?" Tears stream down her face.

"Damned if I know." I turn on my heel to go into the tent and just about run over Stormy. She gives me one hell of a look, and then she sits on another white chair next to Roseanne. Stormy puts her arm around the woman, who buries her face in my girl's chest and sobs.

I don't know. I should be more sympathetic, but I get impatient with emotions. Could be I have trouble with self-pity. Maybe it's that too-well-learned, that "pull yourself up by your own bootstraps" philosophy of the West. My grandmother, who crossed the plains in a covered wagon, would say, "School in your feelings, girl." Guess I inherited more than her genes.

I look around for someplace out of the way for my gun and settle on under the food prep counter, then go and help shovel some garbage into an empty feedbag. Most of the trash is composed of tin cans we'll have to pack out. We build a fire in the outside pit and burn what we can, the tin cans going on last to burn off the food residue. Afterward, we pile the cans on the ground and stomp them flat.

Candace gets into it, snapping her fingers above her head like a Spanish dancer. She is a kick. Candace has grown on me.

I stand to one side and clap in time.

Once the fire burns down, I go back into the tent to see if there is any more garbage to burn.

"God, what pigs those men were!" Rachel scrubs the oilcloth table cover. "I found five pounds of coffee in one of the supply boxes. There's a pot just about ready to drink."

I'm longing for my first cup in days. "Will you marry me?" Then I blush scarlet and mutter, "Oh, God!"

A soft "Sure" comes from beside me, and I glance over to see Rachel with a twinkle in her eye.

Now I pour myself a mug of black coffee. I call over to Stormy, "Want some?"

"Later." Stormy winks at me. "Storm's brewing out there."

"In your dreams." I glance outside and sure enough, the sky has a nasty look.

I say to the women in the tent, "If anybody wants a shower, those bags aren't going to get any warmer. We might have weather this afternoon. I'll rig up one."

We have more takers than bags, so they have to share. We use both our shower stalls in a bathing frenzy. I refill them as they're emptied against the next round.

Karen says, "I am feeling really good about how everyone's taken back our camp."

"Me too." But I am shaken out of my pleasure by a scream. I rush out to see Mark's lovely black mare, nearly white with sweat, charge in circles around the camp. She runs to the corral, raising her head to touch noses with Buck. Red-brown blankets her rump.

The screaming thing is Bridger, yet amazingly on his horse, erupting over the river edge, water running in torrents from him and his horse, wailing something about Mark.

Karen and I run up to him. His horse drops his head, nostrils round and red, sorrel coat dark from sweat and water. Hal's horse, so used to following, rams into the back of the bald face gelding.

Bridger falls off and sits in the dirt bawling. "Mark's dead. Mark's dead. A grizzly ate him." He is howling.

"What happened?" I ask.

Bridger gasps and says, "We was just riding along, and this bear came out of the underbrush."

"Where is Hal?" Karen says calmly.

Bridger looks around, wild-eyed. "He's right here."

"You don't know when he fell off?" I can see he is too shaken to answer coherently. I turn, find Stormy, and say, "Take the biter and get my rifle while I saddle Buck. I'll need that if I come up against the bear." I figure Hal's horse is the only one with strength left since he hasn't been packing Hal.

Bridger clings at me. "Are you going to save Mark?"

"There's no saving Mark, but I might get a chance at Hal. Depending on how far back he is."

Just as I get Buck saddled, Stormy rides the spent horse back with my rifle. She says, "Just let me get my horse, and I'll come with you."

"No. Stay here."

"If you find him, how will you get him back here? At least lead another horse."

"I don't want the hassle of a second horse. It could get spooked."

I fix the scabbard in place and mount up. Skip is ready,

looking up at me with her mismatched eyes. I slip my foot out of the stirrup, pat my leg, and say, "Up."

She takes a mighty leap, hind feet finding the stirrup, and she clambers into the saddle in front of me. I put my arm around her, and we head for the river. After we cross, I slide her to the ground, and we head down the trail.

Buck's ground-eating walk covers the trail in a hurry. We jog where the footing is good.

About an hour goes by and still no Hal. We are getting too close to where I left the deer carcass for comfort. I reach down and unbuckle the scabbard top so I can pull the rifle out in a hurry. I keep an eye on Skip knowing she'll give me warning.

My plan for the bear attack has worked. My guilt in that department is why I have to go after Hal. When I placed the carcass in the brush, the reality of a man devoured by a bear was a distant hope. Now I'm faced with the horror. Bridger had no idea where Hal came off his horse, and I'm praying he got a ways down the trail from the bear before he fell.

But we are getting too close.

I'm as tense as a lynx when Skipper stops in the middle of the track, raises her hackles, and lifts one front leg. A growl comes from the dog like a whisper. I edge up beside her, stand in the stirrups, and peer down the path. Something big is curled up in the dirt. But if it's a bear, it's wearing overalls.

CHAPTER TWENTY-THREE

I ride toward Hal, who holds a hand up to ward off whatever he imagines is approaching. "Hal. Are you hurt?"

He whips around and whimpers. "Oh, my God, it's you. A bear is eating Mark."

"I know. We've got to get out of here. Are you hurt?"

"Yes. I think I broke my wrist. And the damned horse rammed my knee into a tree."

"Can you stand?"

"I'm not sure." He winces as he tries to straighten out his leg. He's at the wrong angle to push himself up while cradling his hand at his chest. I get a blast of the strong smell of urine. He is not the first to piss his pants in fear.

"You'll have to stand in order to get on the horse. Let me help you." *Jesus, he is heavy.* I try to help him up, but he falls back.

"You're going to have to help yourself. And do it fast. I'm worried about that bear coming up the trail."

That got some action out of him. With the aid of a nearby rock for him to step up on, I help him into the saddle. I'd have to lead the horse. It was asking too much of Buck to pack us both. I set off at a jog, but Hal's cries of pain got me to slow to a walk. I keep an eye on Skipper, who crosses back and forth at Buck's heels, glancing to the rear over her shoulder. That worries me some.

After what seems like an eternity, we come to the river crossing. I tie the reins across Buck's neck and send her across, praying Hal won't fall off into the ice water. "Hold on!" I needlessly shout after him. Skip and I stand on the bank, watching the progress. Good old Buck takes him safely across and stands in front of the cook tent.

The horse and Hal are quickly surrounded. Hal slides on his belly down the saddle to the ground, wincing as his feet touch. He is taken into the tent.

I smile to see that Stormy had her horse saddled, and after catching up Buck's reins, rides across to fetch Skip and me. She enters my arms, and we hold each other a long time.

"I was so scared," Stormy says.

"Me too." I sigh a long one. "Jess was right. No rejoicing we're rid of them until we know for sure."

"We're back to square one. Bridger has your gun."

"What? Oh, shit. How did he find it?"

"Roseanne did, actually. She was rummaging around looking for some bear pepper spray and the idiot said, 'What's this doing here?' and held it up. The way he's waving it around, he wants to be king now that Mark's gone."

"I never thought…why didn't I just hide it?" Frustrated and angry, I turn and pace away from Stormy, then spin back to face her. "Damn it to hell."

"It all happened very fast. We were all clustered around Bridger—comforting him, would you believe—when we saw Roseanne hold the gun up. Bridger grabbed it out of her hands, and then Mike jumped him. I think she would have shot him if she had gotten her hands on it. Bridger was pretty freaked that the gun went off, but it was pointed up, so we were all lucky. Took some but not all the starch out of him."

"God damn."

Disappointment with our new reality made me sluggish about rejoining the fray. Slowly I mount Buck, Stormy boosts Skip into the saddle in front of me, and we cross to the other side.

"That's quite a maneuver with your dog," Stormy observes. "Impressed a lot of onlookers when you rode off."

"Could only do that on Buck."

"Why on earth did you risk your life going after Hal? I'd just as soon shoot him," Stormy says in all seriousness.

"Call it guilt. I put that carcass in a place I knew could be a trap for those men riding out. Hoped it would draw a bear. All seems a little too real."

"Did you really? I call that brilliant."

We put the horses away, and I manty my saddle well, hoping Bridger was in such a panic, he never noticed the rifle. I rub down Buck and thank her for her extra work.

Bridger comes toward us, then stops halfway. "Where's my personal gear? You know, my saddlebags. Someone did something with them."

"Well, yeah. After I unsaddled your horse for you, I slung them over there, at the end of the rail." Stormy pointed to the saddle rack.

"Get them for me."

"Get them yourself. I'm sick of taking orders from you like some slave."

I could see this might heat up. "Stormy, let's see what we can do for that black mare."

"Mike and I already washed the wounds, but the slashes are in a place we can't bandage."

The mare stands off by herself, head down and the hind leg under the wounded hip resting on the toe. "She's hurting."

"I put some salve on it to keep the flies off."

"Let's give her some bute for the pain. Did you bring some?"

"Jess has some packed in the first aid kit. She left it with me. I'll get it."

The scene playing out in the cook tent is tragicomic. Barbara has a nursing station set up and is binding Hal's wrist with gauze and a cotton bandage over a splint. Roseanne is metaphorically fluffing pillows under Hal. Her face is wet with tears, and she makes cooing sounds. How can she get this emotionally involved in just a few days? Starved, I guess. She is certainly exhibiting amnesia about Hal's character. Bridger is sitting in the corner with my pistol aimed at everyone.

"Put that damned thing away or you might shoot someone," I tell him.

He grunts, stroking the gun barrel.

The power has shifted, though. We have taken back the cook tent, and no one cares what these men say. Someone has a batch of pancakes in the works, and the oilcloth-covered table is wiped clean with tin plates set around the perimeter. Karen calls out, "First pancake shift, sit down."

"You never have to call me twice." I take up a fork. Roseanne carries a plate to the prone Hal, cutting his pancakes up for him like a baby. She must have helped him out of his soiled pants because he lies under a blanket now. Hal is telling anyone who will listen about seeing Mark fall under the front feet of the grizzly, and the fact I'd come along and saved his life.

I have strong doubt his gratitude will make our lives easier.

"Let's see if we can deal with the pain that mare's feeling," I say to Stormy.

Stormy wipes up the last of the syrup with a piece of pancake, stuffs it into her mouth, and fetches the anti-inflammatory and painkillers from Jess's kit. We smash two big pills into some of the syrup. It's a job getting it into the mare, but most of it goes into her mouth.

Hal's moans are audible from outside. He's saying, "You've got pain stuff for the horse but nothing for me?"

I ask if we have anything for his pain.

Mike snorts. "I'd add to it if I could."

Barbara meets us at the opening of the tent. "I think his wrist is broken. I've done the best I can with it, wrapping it in an Ace bandage with a splint. Gave him a couple of aspirin."

"Are you a nurse?" Stormy asks.

"A physician. One of the few generalists in Seattle."

Karen sighs. "I'm so glad to have you on this trip. Hope nothing else happens that needs your training."

Barbara half smiles. "I agree. I thought I was on vacation."

"Now what?" My so cleverly placed deer carcass has blocked the way out, and now we're stuck with them. "I could escort them past the bear. There wasn't much meat for it to eat and it should leave…"

I stop talking when I remember something with cold chills: Oh, yes, it does. The bear will drag Mark's body into the bushes and feed for a few days. Too dangerous to try to get the men past that point even if they're willing, which I seriously doubt.

"I feel stymied and frustrated. We were so close to getting back our lives," I say.

"Yes. I think we're all feeling that way. Where do we go from here?" Karen asks the question without expecting an answer.

"This excursion is over. We can't carry on with our plans now. Our responsibility is to get everyone back to Benchmark in one piece. The only way out for all of us is to go back the way we came. Bridger and Hal can come with us or not. But we are going out when we are goddamned good and ready."

A growl of thunder echoes over the mountains. I take my cup of coffee outside to watch the lightning. Didn't like the look of it, bouncing across the ridges, moving closer.

I hook my toe out and catch another chair to put my feet on, crossing my legs at the ankles, and I start on the dark brew with a slow smile. I get a few grounds of coffee caught between my teeth, but I'm not going to complain.

Stormy joins me in both the coffee and the storm watching. The aroma is nearly as good as my first sip.

"Ambrosia. I didn't get an inroad on my first cup." I stroke the mug, kiss the rim.

She scoots her chair close to mine. A flash of lightning draws our attention, dancing across the mountains to the west and north. "Looks like dry lightning," I say mostly to myself. "What we don't need right now is a goddamn forest fire."

Stormy, with eyes riveted to the roiling black clouds shot through with ragged bolts of lightning, reaches for my hand.

"Don't get any ideas," I tell her.

A smile blossoms across her face.

CHAPTER TWENTY-FOUR

The morning, filled with such relief and hope, moves to afternoon with its long slanting shadows and a sense of dread and frustration. Everyone seems lethargic and spent. We must change this dynamic and take charge of our lives once again. I speak to Karen, asking her to call a meeting in our sleeping tent. Soon all but Roseanne gather. She won't leave Hal's side, which is really just fine with everyone.

I open the tent flap wide so we can see anyone who approaches, and the talk starts with Mike blasting Roseanne.

"That bitch! The way she sucks up to that disgusting man."

Kamau agrees. "I can't stand to watch them together."

Luci puts her arm around Kamau. "I thought everyone on this trip would be lesbian. She's such a turncoat."

This earns her a strange, eyebrow-raised look from Kamau. "I'm not gender labeled."

An incredulous "What?" Candace has her hands on her hips. "Really! Don't you call yourself Boi?"

Karen steps forward. "I never claimed this to be an all-lesbian trip. No requirement. Was it on your trip form?"

A few of us blush. I glance at Stormy. We are so quick to exclude straight women when they act straight, but if they blend in with us, they're accepted.

I clear my voice and say, "Well, she's difficult, but ours."

"Not mine!" Mike states.

Stormy says, "What do you want to do, Mike? Shun her? For some reason many of us have trouble fathoming, her heart got snagged on Hal. We don't have to understand, but don't you think she's feeling torn up about now? How would you feel if Sue had a broken wrist?"

"I agree," says Barbara. "She is one of our group, and we need to try and understand what she's going through. The main thing we can do is be kind. She sees something in Hal the rest of us can't even imagine, but it's true for her."

Mike sulks. "Well, I'm not having anything to do with her anymore." She looks defiantly at Stormy. "And this isn't anything like Sue and me."

"If I can be so bold," Stormy says, smiling a little to try to soften the next words. "You called on us to understand your impending state of transformation. Some feel as strongly about that as you do about Roseanne. You expect compassion, so you need to give it."

Mike puffs up, sticks her chest out, and says, "That's not the same."

Rachel slips into the conversation. "No. Your situation is politically correct and one we all must support. I actually have more compassion for silly Roseanne than I do for you."

"Wow," Candace says. "We are really pushing it to the PC wall."

Karen says, "We must put our personal feelings aside for now. The only way to get through this is by doing it together."

Mike grunts. "I expected more support than this."

A brief standoff with the eyes takes place.

"Good, that's settled then. Next item of business." Karen snorts like Lily Tomlin. "The men. One injured and one hair-trigger desperate man. I think our trip to the Wall is out. The only thing I can see is to make a journey back to Benchmark and hope no one gets shot in the meantime."

"What are we going to do to convince Bridger that is our only choice?" Rachel says. "My mind comes up blank."

"Neither one of them is going to want to go past the bear, so if Hal wants a doctor and Bridger wants a shot at freedom, they have to come with us." Barbara sounds very reasonable. "The other factor is that my pain management for Hal can be kept at the threshold. By the way, no one tell either one of them that I'm a doctor. That includes Roseanne."

Lightning lights up the tent, followed by a roll of thunder.

"If it clears by morning, I think we need to get humping early, pack what we can and head out. We're running out of feed." Stormy directs her gaze at me for agreement.

"Stormy and I need to round up the horses tonight. In the morning, I'll dump the remaining pellets and grain. Mike, maybe you, Luci, and Candace can help get the riding stock ready while Stormy and I pack the horses with all the personal gear."

"What about Bridger?" Rachel says. "Is Hal fit to ride?"

"He'll have to," Barbara says. "I'll strap his arm down to minimize the trauma."

"Bridger can stay here if he wants, but we're going." Karen's mouth is set, lips firm.

Sometime in the night, I awaken to a distinct smell of burning fir. With all the lightning and thunder, rain never came. Stormy is curled against me and stirs as I slip out of bed. I pull on a shirt and go out to see if I can see flames. The smell of the smoke is stronger, but I can't spot any fire. It's there, though, someplace.

Karen comes out of her tent. In the moonlight, we move closer and whisper our fears.

She says, "The smoke is so pungent."

"Fire usually moves uphill. The wind comes from the west generally, so we could be right in the fire's path," I say while scanning the distance.

"Do you know what time it is? Maybe we should wake everyone."

"I'd guess an hour before dawn. Let's wait. You'd be surprised how far the smell of burning fir can travel. I'll get dressed and go out where I can get a better view."

"Wait for me," Karen says and ducks back into her tent.

Skip watches me from her place, lying across the tent opening, while I dress and pull on my boots. She knows something's up and is not going to let me out of the tent without her. I wait for a minute or two for Karen, who appears with a flashlight. We go past the corrals, horses calling in low voices filled with hope for a ration of hay pellets. The trail back toward the pass gets some altitude, and we should have a clear view of the mountains to the west from there.

Karen and I scramble up the trail, checking back over our shoulders to the big trough in the mountains to the west.

And there it is, not big yet, but a fire burning a red glow at the mouth of the valley, perhaps fifteen or twenty miles away. Not far enough away for comfort at the speed fire can travel in a ten-mile-an-hour wind.

"Time to wake everyone," I say, turning. "This might make a change of plans."

"We'll gather in the cook tent."

I raise a hand to signal I've heard her and keep going straight to Stormy. She jumps up after I tell her. "And get everyone up before you join me."

In the corrals, I roughly sort out the riding and pack animals into separate corrals, then dump four bags of pellets out in the feeders for the saddle horses. No need to be cautious with it anymore, and this might be the last chance these horses have to eat for a while. Women are moving through the trees toward the cook tent, and I join them. We need to make some basic decisions fast, before the heat of the day works to the fire's advantage.

Everyone's talking at once. Bridger is waving the gun around trying to get control of the group.

I yell out, "Listen! We have to act fast. Bridger, put that gun down. There's no time for your theatrics. This is what we've got to do: someone pack all the easy-to-eat food in saddlebags, gather your essentials, like medicine. One blanket each. A wool, canvas, or leather jacket is best. No polyester or fleece, too flammable. Nothing more than we can easily carry. Stormy and I'll run the nonessential horses and mules up toward Gladiator—"

"What do you mean?" Luci is outraged. "Abandon them? No way!"

"The only horses we can manage are the ones we need to ride out over White River Pass. The pack animals will be safe enough going north. They'll be all right until we can come back for them. But right now, get the horses ready. The fire is slow burning in the cool of night, but it could turn into an inferno once the day heats up or a breeze freshens."

"What about all the Decker pack gear? We can't just leave it behind. Jess will be really upset if all that is lost," Stormy says.

"Mike, as soon as we run the packhorses out of the one corral, dig a shallow hole in the center, then shovel dirt over the gear. Get someone to help, and the rest of you saddle the horses. We'll need eleven. Don't know if we have that many saddles, so save out Deckers to make up the difference. Better than nothing."

The sun has risen by the time we leave the cook tent, throwing a murky light.

The pack animals are surly being cut out of breakfast, watching the chosen horses chewing the pellets, and are reluctant to leave. The black mare is the most unwilling to move, but she must go with the others. I get Skipper after them and soon they are heading north up the side valley toward Gladiator. Stormy and I push them a little farther, then make our way back through wafting smoke, visible now.

When we ride into camp, it is utter chaos; people running everywhere. I tell Stormy, "Let's strike one wall tent and roll up the personal gear inside. That might keep everything from getting burnt."

Kamau glances to the west. "Shouldn't we hurry? Let's leave everything and go!"

"This won't take long, and it will pay off if the fire reaches the camp."

We gather up a few helpers and get the tent struck, fold the personal gear inside, and stack it in the bare dirt corral.

The day is heating up with a vengeance. I think we had better get going before that fire blows up. Perhaps I'd taken too much time, cutting it too close betting that the fire won't blow up until midday or early afternoon, but a brisk wind out of the west is fanning the flames.

I call out, "Let's get on the horses."

Roseanne is supporting Hal as he hobbles toward the tie-up rack. "I won't ride that same horse," he swears. His speech is slurred.

Stormy isn't brooking any nonsense from him. "Get on. This is the best horse for you."

"What's going on?" I demand from him, and then turn to Roseanne. "It's like he's drunk."

She says, sheepishly, "He was in so much pain last night, he took one of the horse's pills."

"Jeez," says Stormy. "That's meant for a thousand-pound horse."

"We can't put him in a saddle, he'll just fall off." I think a minute. "Put him on one of the packsaddles, and we'll tie him on. Let's get moving."

We get him onto the back of the biter gelding. He gets tied around the waist, then to the front and back metal loops. "If you fall off this time, no one is coming back for you. Just so you know."

The knuckles of his one good hand are white gripping the front arched loop of the Decker.

I look around and see we're still short a saddle. Luci says, "I'll ride bareback."

She vaults on so neatly, it'd make a trick rider proud.

The fire is visible now, crawling up the sides of the valley as it approaches with a roar. Smoke and sparks fly through the air. The explosive crack of pinecones shooting out ahead of the flames sounds like gunshot.

Everyone's mounted. I climb on, shouting, "Let's ride!" Skipper is ready, right beside me. Horses pick up the urgency, digging into the trail. I glance back over my shoulder. They're all there, Hal in the middle with Roseanne riding behind. Stormy is in the rear.

Bridger is right behind me, the gun in its holster hanging from the saddle horn. He looks over his shoulder at the fire. No more nonsense from him. He's facing a greater fear.

The fire is traveling faster than we are.

CHAPTER TWENTY-FIVE

Smoke thickens the air. The roar of the fire pushes us like a rabid dog. Pinecones pop, exploding in flames, and the heat is intense. We aren't staying ahead with any degree of safety margin. Fire burns uphill, but up is the only way out.

I made a big mistake, trying to get things secured. I was too complacent about the fire, figured we'd have enough time. Should've just left the damned tent up and written off the women's belongings. If I'd known the fire would act up so fast, I might've led everyone up where we graze the horses. We'd be trapped, probably for days, but it was unlikely the fire would travel that way.

At the turn-off for the Chinese Wall, I make a decision. I hold up one hand to stop the riders and call back, "We've got to get up onto bare rock. We can't outrun this fire."

Bridger says, "No. We're going out."

"You're wrong, buster. If you go, you go alone."

The heat from the fire is rising up the valley, pushed by the fire's own wind. "Move it," I shout.

I urge Buck to scramble up the side trail to Haystack as fast as she can go over the rocks and tree roots. I think of Stormy at the end of the line, the fire hot on her heels. The trail has many switchbacks going up Haystack Mountain to the bare rock at the top of the wall. At the bends, I have too good a view of the approaching flames. Stormy is at the end hazing the last riders. I only get a glimpse of her through the smoke as we make the turns in the trail.

The trees get progressively smaller, like saplings, because of the wind along the top of the Continental Divide. At least there is considerably less fuel along the side of Haystack Mountain. We're soon free of the small trees, and the world opens up to solid rock all along the top of the granite uplift.

Smoke fuzzes much of the line of cliff running for miles to the north. It is a breathtaking scene, but not the one I wanted everyone to get, never mind the gasping for oxygen through the smoke.

Riders pack up behind me. "Get off your horses and blindfold them. Take your shirts off and put them across the brow band and over your horse's eyes and nose. Keep a good grip on the reins and try to keep them from panicking. Get down as low as possible, cover your heads with your jacket or a blanket. We'll have to wait here for the fire to pass. And whatever happens, don't let go of your horse's reins."

I take off my jacket and cotton shirt, remove my T-shirt, and fold it over the brow band, draping it over Buck's eyes and letting it hang over her nostrils. Modesty seems out of place here. I see others do the same as I pull my long-sleeved shirt back on. I drape my canvas jacket over my shoulders, ready to pull it over my head while I watch to make sure everyone is following my orders.

The horses are keyed up, some fighting the riders to turn and run, like going back into a burning barn. Steel shoes racketed on the hard rock. I yell out, "Don't go any closer to the edge of the wall. Keep a firm grip on those reins. Stay near me in a bunch. This is as good as it gets." I'm relieved to see Stormy make it through the scrub trees. She rides up next to me, jumps off, and I draw her close.

"I'm so scared, Miles."

"We all are, honey."

The roar of the fire grows, smoke chokes us. Hacking coughs pierce the air. I kneel down, pulling Stormy and Skipper to me, and cover our heads with my jacket. The heat and flames rob the air of oxygen. My throat feels like sandpaper has been run back and forth the length of it. Each breath sears through my windpipe into my heavy lungs.

Skip shivers in fear against my leg. She presses her nose into the space between my chin and shirt collar. I feel her damp breath in short, nervous bursts. The path of the fire is right up over the pass toward Indian Creek. If we'd kept to the trail, we'd be crispy critters right now.

Time is in a stall. Minutes seem endless, fighting for air through the smoke. I take a look at my watch. We left camp at nine thirty, and now it is four in the afternoon.

Cool air mixes with the dusky scent of burning fir trees. I poke my head out to discover fresh air mixed with smoke. I rise to my feet to see the fire has been slowed by the lack of fuel on the pass itself. Small spot fires burn out ahead, but I think the power of the fire is spent.

A few of the women rise to their feet, stunned. A weak twist of a smile comes from Rachel. "We lived through that one."

"I think we should have left earlier," Kamau says with a pointed look at me.

"Well, you're right there," I say with a half-smile.

Someone has helped Hal to the ground where he sits glaring and holding a stick threateningly in front of the biter. He has looped the reins around his good wrist. I guess perhaps the biter got one while Hal was out of it.

Bridger has the damned gun out again, trying to assert

control over the indifferent women. We've all been threatened too much to care.

While everyone is still confused and preoccupied with the fire, I think I might have a chance of disarming him before he shoots someone. I hand Buck's reins to Stormy. "Hold her for me for a minute, okay? Skipper, too. Stay here," I tell the dog.

Stormy quickly turns her head toward me and lifts one eyebrow a little. Not about to tell her what I'm planning, I fake a wracking cough when Bridger turns my direction. When he looks off over the wall, I creep closer. I gather my feet under me ready for a spring. My shoulder hits him at his hips and he goes down. I grab his gun arm trying to get him to drop it, but his grip is firm. I grasp his arm at the elbow and slam it against the rock.

The gun explodes off a shot, and then skitters across the rock and over the side. I hear a cry from one of the women as I grab Bridger around the legs. He kicks free to turn on me, grasping me around my hips. Entwined in long-pent-up hatred, we roll over the ground, my shoulders digging into rough edges of rock.

Bridger locks his legs around mine, and I bite his ear, our embrace mimicking intimacy of a different kind. He grunts, trying for leverage. My shoulder that Bridger bent back on that first day is screaming with renewed pain.

I know I'm way stronger than he expected a woman to be. He hadsnever come up against any woman who could toss a hundred-pound hay bale. More than one.

Suddenly, we both drop over the edge. I gasp, anticipating the long drop.

The fall to a ledge jolts us apart. I woof out the air I'd taken. I grab the rock with one hand, eyes on the place where steel-gray sky meets granite, my feet pushing my body firmly against the back of the ledge. Fear takes the form of ice water on the bottoms of my feet, rising up through my core to the muscles in my jaw.

Bridger rises on one knee, drags his Bowie knife from its sheath, and crouches to jump me, with one hand braced like a spider on the rock.

No way can I back away from him. I sweep my foot in an arc, kicking his supporting hand out from under him. His elbow hits hard. With a roar like a bear, he stands up, then shoots an arm out for balance, his hand gripping the knife like a lifeline. He waves the other arm in a circle, and slowly, as though being plucked from the cliff rim by an unseen force, Bridger plunges backward into open air. His howling scream, filled with all our deepest fears, lasts a very long time.

I unlock my body and crawl over the ledge up to solid earth, shaking. I rest my cheek on the hard rock and marvel at the rise and fall of my chest against the stone. My ears are ringing and my chest burns. I take in short bursts of panting breath.

Back where everyone is gathered, all the attention is on someone lying in the center of the circle of women.

CHAPTER TWENTY-SIX

S he's been shot! Karen's shot," Stormy cries, her mouth working in agony. She stoops beside Karen with one hand on Skipper's collar.

One of the horses is pawing wildly. Others are snorting and shaking their heads.

I run to them, say to Mike, "Take the horses. Lead them back into the nearest trees and tie them up. Get everyone to tie up their horses. We don't need them panicking and running over the cliff."

When I turn back, Barbara is kneeling beside Karen.

I stand hulking, feeling helpless. "How bad is it?"

"There's a lot of blood."

"What happened?"

"When you knocked the gun out of Bridger's hands, it went off."

"Oh, God!" I put my hands over my face. *How can it get any worse?*

"Did anyone bring a first aid kit?" Barbara says.

Stormy stands up. "I've got one in my saddlebag."

"Get it!" Barbara barks. "And get that small blue pouch from my saddlebags."

That command brings us all out of our stupor. I fetch my

bedroll tied behind my saddle. We all want to help, even if it is a small way. "Will she be all right?" Luci says.

Karen's soft voice is shaky. "I'll be fine. Just have to rest a minute."

"I've got the bleeding stopped. I don't think the bullet lodged in her."

"Where is she hurt?" I kneel beside them. Stormy comes up, crouches, then opens the kit and sets it beside Barbara. We all look at the pitiful supplies inside. Some gauze bandages. A pair of forceps, iodine and salve. Lots of Band-Aids.

"Help me pull her jeans off. I can't cut them or she'll have nothing." Barbara unzips the fly and gently draws the jeans down to expose the wound in her thigh. This girl is not going to be riding. The bullet cut a path through the muscle on the outside of her leg. This is going to hurt like the dickens. Barbara takes the forceps and removes some shreds of fabric from the wound, then tears open three large square bandages and places them overlapping the torn flesh. I hand her the gauze, which she wraps tightly around until the roll runs out.

"I need a shirt I can tear up." All of us unbutton and begin peeling off our shirts. "Clean. Cotton. You won't be getting it back."

She reached out for mine. I hand her my knife, and she tears the shirt into long strips to bind Karen's leg. "Bring more blankets and try to make her comfortable. I've given her a couple of oxycodone."

"Those weren't in the kit," Stormy says.

"I always carry some with me." Barbara stands and motions me to join her. We walk off a little ways. "She's not going to be able to ride."

"I can see that. We have to get her out of here," I respond.

Barbara takes a breath to argue with me, but I hold up

one hand. "I'll make a travois. Indians used them to transport people too old or injured to ride. Won't work on this trail, but it will on the main one. Buck can pull it, she's totally trustworthy."

"How will we get her down to that point?"

"Make a stretcher out of poles and blankets."

Barbara places one hand on my arm and looks me right in the eye. "I knew you'd know what to do."

"She won't be comfortable, but it'll get her out of here with the least pain and harm."

On our return, Hal demands pain pills from Barbara.

"Sorry, I don't have that many. You'll just have to tough it out."

"You scum, can't take it, can you?" Mike spits on him.

"Mike, what the hell!" Rachel says, shocked.

He sneers at us. Perhaps he thought it was a smile. "Then make them give me more of that horse medicine."

Stormy snorts and turns her back on him. "I'm saving that for the horses."

I think Hal can still be dangerous, so I make a decision. "Hal, I thought you might like to know that the man you shot back in your home state, well, he's going to make it. In the hospital. We heard it on the news."

I see Karen's eyes fly open. She is still with it enough to know I'm laying out a whopper. Stormy whips her head around to study me.

"You didn't kill him, Hal."

Relief floods him, and Roseanne clutches him and kisses him. "We'll be able to be together. You won't have to go to jail, like you thought. Or at least, not for very long."

I catch Stormy's eye, point my lips to one side, and we both move over toward the horses. "That's a lie," she says, hissing it out.

"You are so right. You have any better ideas for defusing him? Now we don't have to worry about turning our backs on him."

I get a couple of blankets from behind the saddles and call to Mike. "Help me make a stretcher. Does anybody by any chance have an ax?"

"Just a hatchet," Mike says.

I sigh with relief. "Great. We'll need it. You've just earned your Boy Scout badge."

Mike gives me a wink.

We retrace the trail back where the trees are not so twisted from the wind. Some areas are totally burnt and still hot. Islands the fire didn't touch stand out sharply, and we find the poles we need there. One pole is scorched, but that's all right.

My heart sinks as I see how hot everything still is. There's no way we can get out of here today. We'll have to wait overnight for the burned areas to cool down.

Pretty soon we have a workable stretcher, and I make it so we can remove it from the travois when the trail gets steep, narrow, or rough.

Karen is asleep when we return. We have a little conference to work out how we'll manage transporting her down to the main trail. I break it to everyone that we'll have to spend the night on Haystack and suggest we try for crossing the pass early tomorrow morning.

"I'm worried about taking any more time than we must," Barbara says.

"We can't travel in the dark, and that's only a couple of hours away. We're bound to run into some hot spots we can't cross or go around. Is there a chance she'll be stronger in the morning?"

"Yes," Barbara says, considering. "But she's lost a lot of

blood. The body can only take so much pain. I'll need to dole out the pills very carefully."

"Once we get the pass behind us we'll need to rest. From the point I'm thinking about, it's only about fifteen miles to Benchmark. I can send a rider out ahead to arrange a medevac helicopter to pick her up and take her to Great Falls."

"What kind of time frame is this?"

I stare at the wall, the high drop ending in a scree slope, built up over centuries. "If we really push it, we should be across the pass tomorrow. We'll need a break at Indian Creek of a couple of hours for the horses to grab some grass and for riders to rest. I can't quite remember if a medevac can land there. If so, we can wait. Maybe help could arrive in late afternoon."

Barbara groans. "I'm worried about her. And we have two injured members of our party now. That will slow us up. Hal is being a pain about his pain, wanting drugs for it."

"I'll take care of Hal. Keep him away. Maybe we should just dope him up with the horse painkiller."

Barbara gives me an odd expression. "Easy to overdose?"

"Not what I was thinking, but we might be able to manage him better."

"What's the dose?"

"Two grams, or pills, for a one-thousand-pound horse."

"Give him one-fourth. That should keep him quiet, but hopefully not kill him."

I nod. "I'm so glad you're on this trip."

"Lucky thing, eh? For everyone but me." Her eyes are red and tearing from the smoke.

I take her arm and give it a little squeeze, "You're great."

I step closer to the group. "Gather around, everybody. I hate to tell you this, but we have to spend the night here."

Groans at the expected hardship are hard to ignore. "Yes, it will be a long night, but we can't go until morning."

Kamau points toward the pass. "It has mostly burned out. Why can't we just—"

I interrupt her. "There are too many hot spots and it will be dark soon."

Luci complains, "This rock is going to get very hard."

"Unsaddle the horses and put all the saddles here on the rock, then bring the pads to where you want to sleep. Hips to shoulders. I'm afraid that's as good as it gets."

I study the group, assessing the strongest members. "At first light, we all need to take turns carrying Karen down to where the main trail joins this one. When we get there, I'll fashion a travois. We'll need to carry her over rough places on the trail. Are you all up for that?"

I make the count. "We have six. That includes you, Roseanne."

"I can't leave Hal. He needs me."

"Sorry. You have to pull your weight. Hal will be unable to fall off the horse once I get through with him."

I walk over to where I can see the progress of the fire. Smoke swirls the air but is lessening.

Stormy says to the group, "Bring your water bottles. We've got plenty of granola bars for dinner." She laughs. "Yum."

Complaints accompany the slap of saddle pads hitting the rock. I say to them, "It won't be fun tonight, but you'll get through it. Do some creative visualization that you're on a Girl Scout campout."

"Oh, that's helpful," Luci says with a hint of sarcasm.

CHAPTER TWENTY-SEVEN

We awake to a clear cold dawn. Horses have been coughing all night, deep, hollow barks. I am so stove up, I can hardly stand straight. After some slow stretches, trying like crazy to keep my moans and grunts to a respectable level, I nod to Mike. "Guess we need to get going."

Stormy says, "I'll get everyone up and help them saddle."

"Right. We'll need a head start." I stretch out my complaining arm, my shoulder shooting pains down to my fingers.

I go to Karen and gently say, "Are you ready for this roughhousing?"

She gives me back a slow, weak smile. "Do I have an alternative?"

I shake my head.

"Then let's do it."

Barbara is taking care of Karen. "I gave her two pain pills about twenty minutes ago. Should be kicking in."

Mike and I lead off carrying Karen. Smoke screens the trail and trees like the mountain's shroud. My eyes burn trying to see the way ahead, and I blink constantly like a contact lens wearer in a sandstorm. Mike hacks as though she's a twenty-year confirmed smoker. Quite a pair.

The switchback turns are steep and awkward carrying the stretcher. On one double back, my boots shoot out from under me, and I try to control the stretcher's fall onto my chest. Mike looks back over her shoulder. "You okay?"

"Been lots better."

I feel a quick lick on my face. Skip, checking me out and trying to reassure me. I smile and rub her neck.

Mike lowers her handles at the head end to the ground. Karen opens her eyes, murmurs something unintelligible. Thanks to Barbara's pills, she is not feeling the jolts along the rough scree trail. Her eyes close, and she frowns.

Mike lifts the end of the stretcher that lies on my chest, and I crawl out from beneath it. These damn cowboy boots. Like roller skates. Wish I had a pair of riding sneakers like Stormy wears. Good for riding or walking.

As we approach the tree line, we have to do a few detours around hot spots, flames using up the last of the fuel. When my arms feel like burning embers, I call ahead. "We need relief."

Rachel and Kamau dismount, and we switch. I get Skipper to ride in the saddle with me. Don't want her to burn her pads. She presses her body back against me, claws gripping the fork of the saddle.

By the time we reach the cross trail, we have all been used up. Karen begins moaning about this time. Barbara comes to sit with her, bathing her face in cool water, while Stormy and I cut two travois poles. They're about twenty feet long and around two to three inches in diameter. I want them as light as possible for Buck's sake and as flexible and springy as possible for Karen's. It's hard to find just the right poles and we end up finding one lodgepole and one aspen that fit the bill.

I cross them at Buck's saddle horn and lash them together, tie them loosely to the cinch rings, and draw the poles back well behind her hocks and strap them so they'll be somewhat flexible. I notch a place and lash one pole where Karen's feet will reach to help her stay in place on the angled travois.

When all is ready, we lift Karen out of the stretcher, set her on the ground, and then fix the stretcher to the travois poles.

"How's she holding up?" I ask Barbara.

Barbara stands, sways a bit, and puts one hand to her forehead. "Not enough sleep lately. I wish we could give her a transfusion."

I reach for her arm to steady her and search her eyes. She is worried.

"So far, so good."

"Yes," she says.

Stormy and I lift Karen back onto the stretcher and add some straps to keep her from slipping down: one at her arms and another at her hips. I get on Buck, and we set out. With one flash back of her ear, the mare walks along steady as a plow horse.

I glance at my watch, and my heart sinks. Nine thirty. This has all taken so much time. We've got to cross the pass yet and then get down where it's level, the air is better, and the horses have grass. They've had nothing to eat since yesterday morning.

The last part of the trail before the pass is grueling, steep with rocks like ball bearings. Once we get to the top, we quickly take the stretcher off the travois to get her down over the rock steps. The stink of the fire surrounds us, and a fair amount of smoke rises around us, but on the far side, I can see the fire didn't cross the pass.

Hacking coughs are a constant. I feel pretty queasy, and my eyes are running.

We reach the first meadow about one in the afternoon, pillows of alder brush set in a blanket of tall grass. I'm on the skittish, watchful side remembering this is not very far from where we saw the feeding bear. Stormy and I hobble some of the horses, put a few on a picket line, and turn the rest loose. We'll switch them later. They make a beeline for a small stream nearby. By the time we're done, someone has a fire started.

We all look spent and tired. Rachel has a little pot in her kit, one of those backpacker jobs. We fill it and start it heating for the first of many times.

Rachel sets tea bags out on a rock. "Use one per pot. It'll be weak." She smiles apologetically.

"But hot," I say, with a wink. "Anyone have any sugar?"

Luci, sitting by the fire, slaps her knees. "By God, I think I've got some." She goes to her saddlebags, rummages a minute, and comes back with a bag of those little packets you get in restaurants.

"Life savers," I say with a grin. "You know, now's the time for those. We need a sugar fix. We can have some oatmeal gruel, and as far as food's concerned, we should be out of here and eating at a café by the next time we're hungry."

I hand Stormy the first cup. "Are you able to just go on? I know you're as tired as the rest of us."

"Sure. Once I refuel and my horse gets a few mouthfuls of grass, I'll head out."

Candace says, "Honestly, I'd kill for a chocolate bar."

I rustle up a grin. "I feel the same about coffee."

"Bite me." Candace smiles.

Rachel approaches Stormy and me. "Listen, I don't want to horn in or anything and, Stormy, you have a really nice, fit horse, but I'd just like to offer to ride to get help. Kestrel is fit to travel at speed, and I can leave now."

"That's a thought. But you haven't even had tea or oatmeal, and Kestrel hasn't rested." Stormy leans over to pour some tea for Rachel.

"We can go without it. Benchmark is soon enough to rest." Rachel takes the tea and swigs it down. Coughs puncture the silence. The smoke has choked us all day, even making swallowing the tea hard.

"We'll need a medevac." I lower my voice to a whisper. "And somebody with handcuffs."

"No problem. I can make it to Benchmark in way under two hours, by three o'clock."

"Let's see if Luci will part with her iPhone. It has a GPS. Mark our place here for the medevac. I'm sure it's good enough for them to land."

"Okay, let's catch up all the loose horses and put them on the picket line so they don't follow you," Stormy says.

The horses aren't keen on being caught up, so we have to walk a couple of them down. I don't have anything to tempt them with either, and they know it.

Luci and Kamau are napping, forming a blanket-covered bundle. I reach down to gently shake Luci. "I hate to wake you. We need your phone."

"I checked. Still no bars." Luci covers her head with the blanket again.

"We need it for the GPS so we can tell the helicopter where to land," I say in a soft voice.

"Oh." Luci stares blankly at me for a moment. I figure she is trying to remember where she stashed it. She throws the blanket back and tucks it around Kamau again, then hobbles barefoot to her bag and fishes her phone out. "The battery is probably on its last legs, so don't use it until you have to. Turn it on this way." She explains how to use the thing.

I nod a few times like I understand, then say, "I'm sending Rachel over to hear it from you." I was lost shortly after "here's how you turn it on."

At the sound of approaching hoofbeats, I look up to see Stormy walking and Rachel on her white horse. I motion toward Luci. "The telephone."

"You are so retro." Stormy laughs and saunters over to Luci. They bend their heads together and shortly Stormy nods, handing it to Rachel, who places it inside her jacket's chest zip pocket.

"All set?" Rachel says.

Stormy nods. "The GPS is set for this location."

While Stormy takes care of the phone biz, I hold Kestrel's reins and run my fingertips in the groove under her jaw. I scratch some bug bites, and the mare grunts with pleasure.

Rachel smiles down to me. "Ready to go. Equipped with technology and a terrific breakfast." She holds up a granola bar.

"Your mare seems better rested than the rest. Those Arabs recover fast." What I didn't say was how much I wanted to go with her. Just ride away from Karen's pain, complaints about the lack of food, hard ground, and a bad night's sleep. Or deal with Hal.

I reach out to her, and she touches my palm with her fingers and is gone. The contact is strangely intimate and erotic. As Kestrel trots away, a couple of equines call after her.

They slow to a walk where the trail enters the firs. Rachel will walk five minutes, trot five until the mare is loosened up and warm, and then she can ride fast wherever the trail's footing is good. I feel this inexplicable loneliness as the white horse shadows to gray into the dark firs, then disappears.

I reluctantly turn to go back to our encampment and see an odd look on Stormy's face as she watches me. We look deeply into each other's eyes. "Come here," I say, putting my arms around her.

Mike stokes the fire, pours some water in the gruel pot, and sets it by the flames. I glance over toward Barbara and the prone Karen. Barbara catches my eye and shakes her head a little. I motion her to join me.

In a barely audible voice, Barbara says, "How soon might it be possible to get her medical help and an IV? And how far do we have to take her?"

"We don't have to take her any farther. Rachel will get to Benchmark in less than two hours and can call in our position here so a helicopter can pick her up."

"So you think the paramedics will come here before dark? We just need to last that long."

"That should do it."

"I can't get Karen to drink enough fluids during the times she's conscious. She's worried about having to get up to pee."

"She needs fluids."

"We all need food. Let's put something together."

We press Rachel's pot into service again to make oatmeal with dried fruit. With ten stomachs to feed, we need to make four pots of gruel. I want to make sure everyone is satisfied because this is the last hot meal we'll have.

Hal says something I don't catch. I'd forgotten about him, but his wheedling drawl startles me. The bastard is demanding some of the pills from Barbara. I get up and walk over to where he is lying. I have a strong urge to kick him on his bad knee. I pull air deep inside while he lies there and stares up at me with just a bit of fear, which I enjoy. His voice has a whine running along the edge. "What are you going to do?"

"Karen's hurt because of you men." I say the word "men" as though it is the ugliest word in the English language. "So I don't want to hear any crap about wanting what she needs. You got it?" I turn on my heel and stomp back to the fire.

Roseanne scurries over to me after a few minutes of whispering with Hal. "Please, Miles, he is in so much pain. It breaks my heart."

"You know what breaks my heart, Rosy?" Her big brown eyes are so earnest with the eyebrows slightly raised. I wait in vain for the shake of her head. "Seven other women made this trip expecting that we'd take good care of them, that they would be safe. That man," I dipped my head in Hal's direction, just in case she is confused about which one, "and his pals made our lives a living hell. Quite frankly, my dear, I don't give a damn if he's hurting. In fact, the more he hurts, the happier I am."

"Wow." Roseanne's eyes get bigger, if that is possible. "You're really angry, aren't you?"

I turn away from her. "Damn straight. Just leave me alone. And Barbara, too. If I hear him or you trying to get drugs from her again, I'll tie him to a tree a hundred yards away. Better yet, each of you a hundred yards apart."

I'm not sure I like the smile on my face.

"You say, bitch." Kamau steps up to me with a nod of approval, chocolate eyes dancing.

Stormy catches my eye. "Let's do a prayer circle for Karen. We need to give to her what is most important to her and what she'd do for us."

"You are absolutely right. Come on, everyone, let's gather around Karen and show her we love her."

This time, I'm less reluctant to sit in a circle with these other women. No one says anything or leads a prayer, and I'm relieved. We hold her in our hearts, in the light we create for her.

Later, everyone is napping. I'm jealous, but we'll have to get moving again because it is three o'clock, and the helicopter could arrive anytime in the next half hour.

"Everyone can sleep tomorrow," Barbara says, rising to her feet. "I'll wake the sorry bunch." She smiles at me, then adds, "I only have one pain pill left. I want to cut it close and still not get too far behind the pain."

While we're talking I glance up over her shoulder and see a dark shape leaning over Karen. I grab Barbara's arm and she spins to look. "Bear?" she whispers out in one exploded exhale.

Hal is rummaging in Barbara's medical kit.

"Hal!" We dash to Karen's side.

"What are you doing?" Barbara takes hold of his arm. His hand moves rapidly to his mouth. "No!" Barbara shouts and grabs his jaw. I jump on him, too, knocking him to the ground.

"The bastard took her pill," Barbara says, trying to force his jaw open. I hold onto his head, prying at his jaw, but we see him swallow once, then rapid swallows. He smiles with his lips pressed tight.

I haul off and hit him with my closed fist, wanting to shove that smile down his throat, too. He, amazingly enough, looks surprised.

"What'd you do that for?" He fingers the place that will be purple tomorrow.

"You goddamned lowlife." I spin toward Roseanne, who is peering out over the top of a blanket. "You proud of your gentle, sweet man now?" I ask her, feeling cruel. I'd like to hurt her for caring about this scum of the earth.

I turn back to Hal's smug expression. Never before have I felt such violence toward another person, and it scares me. I have to walk away from him.

I put one arm around Barbara, who is stricken. But I'm shaking, and she's the one who calms me. "Now, now. We're going to get through this. When the medevac gets here, they'll have IV pain medication."

"How long does she have from the pills in her system now?"

"No more than an hour. I have plenty of aspirin I was giving to Hal, but I can't use it with Karen because it's a blood thinner."

I go from blanket to blanket, shaking anyone still napping. "Get up! We need to get cracking. Get your horses saddled— Mike, you and Candace help everyone, okay? Come to the fire for oatmeal, and then we need to gather in that meadow so we can be seen. Once Karen is loaded, we need to ride to Benchmark, and this time I'm going to ride as fast as the trail will let me."

I go to Buck, rig the travois, and soon we are all on our way to the meadow's edge.

CHAPTER TWENTY-EIGHT

We will wait for the helicopter at the boundary of an open field. My stomach growls. Not wanting to take the time, I'd passed on the oatmeal gruel. I pull a granola bar out of my pocket, take one look at it, and put it back. My throat is no match for all those oat edges, sharp as razor blades.

When everyone is gathered, I bark out orders. "I want everyone to tie their horses well to those trees over there." I point to a small aspen grove with a screen of firs between them and the meadow. "I want you to make sure your horse is secure, because they will freak out to see a whirlybird come in to land."

I help unload Hal, dropping him to the ground. He lies there like a lump. "Roseanne, you tie up both of your horses. No! Leave him there for now. I'm tired of doing everything for both of you."

I turn to Karen, who meets my gaze with eyes dull with pain.

"It won't be long now."

Mike and I lift her off the travois for the last time and settle her on soft grass to wait for the medics. Barbara is right by her side. Karen is pale, her face tight. I touch her shoulder. "How are you holding up?"

She manages two words. "All right." I know she's lying.

Stormy and I remove the travois from Buck and set it to one side. I lead her over to join the other horses, then loosen the cinch and scratch along her belly, her favorite place. "I've used you hard the last few days," I tell her. "Soon you'll have a nice vacation with plenty of hay."

Skipper lies down next to her, knowing I won't leave without my horse.

A thump-thumping sound announces the arrival of the helicopter, and I run out to the meadow and wave my arms. It circles once before settling down.

Two medics jump out with kits. "Where is she?" one of them says, not wasting any time.

"Over here." I take them to Karen. Barbara talks with them while I stand to one side. They immediately clean her arm and start an IV. One of the medics looks over her shoulder and hands me the bag to hold. I step up and take it.

The other medic lifts the blanket to check the dressing. "Looks good. I've given her something for pain, but we can transport."

I point to Hal. "We've got a problem with that man over there. He's wanted for murder. Can you secure him and get him out to the authorities?"

"What's the matter with him?"

"He has a broken wrist, so handcuffs might be a problem."

"He's violent?"

"Not so far, but he could be."

"I'm sorry. We have no way to secure him in transit. You'll need to deal with him, at least until Benchmark. We can have a sheriff waiting for you there."

"Oh, I was hoping we'd get rid of him."

"Sorry," she says again. "Let's get our patient transferred to our stretcher." The other medic runs to the helicopter. The pilot cuts the engine and comes to help him. They soon have Karen loaded, and we all stand and watch them lift off and disappear down the valley.

"God, what a relief," Barbara says. "Now what?"

"We get it together and ride the rest of the way out."

"I'm already so exhausted. How long do you think it'll take?"

"We can get back in three hours if we push it hard. By seven tonight. I'd hate to go slower than that, or we'll be riding in the dark."

Stormy says, "You know, I never got to see the Chinese Wall." A chorus of agreement.

"Talk to Karen when she's healed. Maybe we can do this again. Been too much fun, eh?"

Luci laughs. "Quite an experience. These wild mountains. I don't imagine the horrible part could ever happen again."

"I agree. I'd be up for it if Karen is. Well, I'm thinking about that café in Augusta." And Rachel. I know she made it because the medevac arrived, but I wonder how she is. I check my watch. "Four thirty? Hard to believe. Let's ride."

We get to Benchmark worn out, but at least a sheriff's rig meets us at the corrals and takes Hal off our hands. Roseanne hovers near while the sheriff's deputy tells Hal he is being arrested for the death of the DNR official.

Hal looks back and forth between the officer and me. He shouts, "But he didn't die!"

The deputy snaps the cuffs on Hal's ankles.

He slowly turns his body toward me as he gets it. "You lied to me."

I give him a little satisfied smile and nod.

The deputy asks if the cuffs are comfortable, then says, "Your wife has been calling the station nonstop…"

"What? Your wife!" Roseanne catapults herself into the

middle of the action, screaming at Hal. "You told me about how your wife died three years ago and how lonely you are. You bastard!"

He is unceremoniously stuffed into the sheriff's rig before Roseanne can scratch his eyes out. The drugs have worn off and he is complaining and moaning once again, but now he also pleads, "Keep her away from me."

They drive away, Roseanne raging nonstop about what a patsy she was, kicking dirt with the toe of her boot. We all give her lots of space.

Everyone helps unsaddle the horses and lets them loose into the corral. Jess, who arrived in the sheriff's car, unlocks the sliding door of the big trailer, and we get hay. She says to me, "I'll let them rest here tonight, then take them home in the morning."

"Might as well. We may not get back in to retrieve the rest of the horses for a while. And providing everything is not burned to a crisp, the horses up the valley can haul everything out. Will you come yourself or send Stormy?"

Jess laughs. "That nickname is sticking. Don't know when I'll be free yet. When do you think that might be?"

"I'll have to check with the ranger district. Maybe a couple of weeks before they clear us to enter the forest."

I check that the water for the horses is good, pleased to see Rachel's white mare in her little solar-powered electric corral. I toss her some hay too, then stash the saddles in Jess's trailer and get ready to go. Couldn't find the keys to Karen's van. We check her saddlebags and then rummage through all the personal gear.

We didn't find any keys, but we did find about seven hundred thousand dollars in Bridger's saddlebags.

Candace begins the speculation by saying, "Listen, it is totally hopeless to find who this money belongs to. We don't even know Bridger's last name. I think the money should go to Karen. She's had a rough time, and I know these trips are always operating on a shoestring. Honestly, I'll bet she's never put anything aside for retirement."

"One hell of a tip," I say. "Nice fantasy, but I'm sure they'll figure out who Bridger is. There must be enough remains at the bottom of the Chinese Wall to get a DNA sample."

"Then what? Really, he probably stole it from somebody." Candace is sticking her lower lip out in a caricature of a pout.

"Do not covet this money, Candace. Won't happen."

In the end, everyone piles into my horse trailer along with Skipper, and I drive my cargo to Augusta. Driving the truck is like getting on a carnival ride, hurtling down the road at the unbelievable speed of thirty-five miles an hour, with a nightmarish sense of lack of control.

I pull in to the hotel parking at the side of the building, get out, and swing the horse loading door open wide. The women pile out, looking stunned.

"God!" Luci says. "So that's what horses go through. What an experience."

Rachel comes out the front door and up to us. She is looking so good. "What a sorry bunch. Come on in and take a hot shower. We've all got rooms for tonight."

"No need to flaunt your sweet-smelling body and shining hair to all the rest of us scumbags," Luci says with a big smile. "Have you got my phone? Great. First thing I'm doing is charging this baby."

Right there in front of the hotel, I put my arms around Rachel and hug her tight. "Thank you, for everything."

"It's all over, isn't it?" Her voice has a husky purr. "How's Karen?"

"Yes. It's over. One of the first things I want to do is call the hospital."

The showers run nonstop, probably using up the landlord's profit in hot water.

After a meet-up with everyone, I make a few phone calls and manage to change flights for the ones who want to leave the next day. Kamau, Luci, and Candace all want to stay until their scheduled flights. The hotel could accommodate them.

With everyone gathered around listening, I call the hospital and talk to Karen. She sounds good. Once the wound was cleaned, she didn't need surgery, just lots of fluids and pain control. She remembers putting the keys to the van in her zipped jacket pocket. She calls out to a nurse, "Could you tell me what happened to my personal belongings?"

I can hear the nurse mumble, then Karen say, "Yes that's it."

Into the phone, she says, "Miles, they're here!"

I told her I'd come get them first thing in the morning.

After an indescribably delicious hamburger, followed by some too-sweet cherry pie that slides down my gullet like a dream, I order a second hamburger for Skip. "Hold the mustard and lettuce," I say.

Skip wolfs it down about the same way I did. She goes back to curl up beneath the horse trailer, and I bring her a bowl of water.

Stormy takes my arm. "Let's go up to our room."

I follow her up the stairs, marveling at how easy it is to forget how to negotiate them.

She fumbles the key in the lock and drops it to the bare boards. We both go after it, my hand over hers as she clutches the key. My body feels like it has transformed into a hot wave that will crest on her like salt water, sinking to her depths.

Once we've taken our long-awaited hot showers and returned to our room, I lock the door and add the chain, just because I can. I flip the covers back, undressing the bed. We fall naked across the sheets in each other's arms, relief at our present safety bringing me close to tears.

We linger on the bed, touching each other after we have been thoroughly satisfied, and then we dress with clean clothes from our bags.

"I called my parents," she says. "I told them I want to go back to school. I applied on a whim this spring and learned right before this trip that I'd been accepted for veterinary school at Pullman, Washington. They were overjoyed. Guess they'd given up on my wanting any higher education."

I knew what this meant. I'd see very little of her once she got into college. "You'll make a great veterinarian. I'm very pleased for you."

"Miles, I want you to know that spending this time with you has been, will always be, a time…"

I laugh. "Oh, can it, girl. We had fun, didn't we?"

Stormy looks so relieved it hurts in a way. "I didn't know what you thought would happen now, you know, after the trip."

"That you'd come live with me on the ranch? We'd get married? Hell, no. I'm a realist if I'm anything. Not to say I won't crawl into bed at night and think of you for a while."

"I can drive over some weekends. It's only about six hours from the school." She fiddles with the knobs on the bedspread. "The age difference doesn't matter, not to me."

"It would. You'll meet some nice girl at vet school, and I'll be part of your history. You'll tell your girl about that time in the Bob." Couldn't help it, my gut crunched.

She murmured something and snuggled close.

"I told you about Jane. Well, you've lightened my heart. Made it possible to love again, and that's a good thing."

"Let's go get an ice cream cone."

"Oh, baby. Now you're talking."

When Stormy and I walk back into the old clapboard two-story hotel that evening, we find the small living room–like lobby filled with our traveling companions. The air crackles with the energy only intense relief from strain can bring.

Rachel offers us some wine. "Join us. We're rehashing our adventure."

"And really, have some of these chocolates. Honestly, I never thought I'd get enough, but I'm bordering on being sated." Candace pats her stomach.

"Thanks." I smile at this woman I'd grown fond of. "Don't mind if I do."

Stormy says, "We called Karen."

"How is she?" Barbara says.

"She sounds great. We asked her if she'd want to do the trip again. She didn't commit, but I think we might talk her into it."

"Just so long as we don't have any men to contend with," Luci comments.

We all freeze, then turn and look at Mike.

"That's right. Next year I might not be eligible," Mike says, with one arm around the myopic Sue.

"Oh, hell. We might be able to make an exception. An honorary woman." I laugh, defusing the moment.

"We can take this as an opportunity to look at our rigid view of gender," Kamau puts in. "If we choose, we can all be bois." She glances over at Luci. "And some bitches."

Luci melts under her gaze.

"Where's Roseanne?"

"She got a lift to Great Falls with one of the guests here. Left blaming us for everything. She was pissed as hell you lied to Hal and equally mad he lied to her about his wife," Rachel says.

"Far as I could see, it was the only way to make him less desperate. Manageable."

Kamau snorted, wonderfully boi-like. "I don't give a hang if she blames us for Hal's problems. If she can't see he got himself into that mess, she's a goner. She'll be one of those dumb bitches relocating to a new town whenever he's moved to a new federal prison."

"That was such a shitty thing to do, stealing Karen's drugs." Luci gave a little shudder. "Pour me some more wine, darling."

Sue asks, "Any idea when our personal packs will be recovered?"

"There's the problem of when we can travel into the Bob and bring out the pack animals and anything that's not burnt up," Jess says, "so you may need to wait a while to get your things."

Jess has changed. She's not issuing orders; she's simply opening up a topic of conversation, inviting solutions.

I take a sip of wine. "Forest Service will tell us when we can go back in. Might be as long as a couple of weeks."

"What about the stock? Is there enough feed up that valley?" Jess scoots to the front edge of her chair.

"By two weeks, the grass will be getting pretty short. I'll make some phone calls in the morning and see if I can move things along."

"Do you mind? Can you go back in for them?"

Stormy and I do some eye contact. "You up for it?"

"Sure. So, I'll take my horse to your ranch."

I smile to think I'll have another week or so of Stormy.

"Do you need me back at your place, Jess?"

Jess gives Stormy a sharp eye, including me in the scrutiny. "No. If you want to hang out with Miles until the horses can be brought back, that's okay."

Stormy announces her plan to go back to school. "So, Jess, it doesn't look like I'll be working for you this fall and winter."

"Sorry to hear that, Stormy. You'll be hard to replace."

I catch Rachel glancing at Stormy, with the tail end slipping over to me.

I continue with the business at hand. "Personal gear will need to be shipped to each guest. If it isn't burned to a crisp, that is." I squint up my eyes in a lame effort to soften this information.

"Yes, I'll talk to Karen about that. Good. Everything's settled." Jess sits back in her chair. "I'll load up the riding horses and take them back tomorrow. Marty can come up and haul the pack animals and your mare home when you get in, Stormy. Just give her a call when you get back to Benchmark, and she'll come up the next morning."

"Sounds like a plan. I'll head out early to see Karen and get the keys, and we'll have some shuttling to do to get all of you to the airport."

"Oh, but Miles, Kamau, and I can drive them in. Barbara, Mike, and Sue are the only ones flying out tomorrow afternoon," Luci says. "I think we'd enjoy lunch in Great Falls and seeing what the clothes shops have to offer."

Kamau rolls her eyes and smiles indulgently.

"I, of course, am heading out to the fast rivers, past Benchmark. Candace wants to learn fly fishing, so we're going together." Rachel says. I can't help it; my eyebrows shoot up. "Remember? I drove here from my ranch."

"Yes," Kamau says, "Then Luci, Candace, and I can take the van back when we fly out."

"You are all so organized," I say.

"I plan on hanging out until I get sick of fishing. That could be when the snow flies."

I smile at Rachel's enthusiasm. "You have someone to run your ranch for you?"

"Actually, I do. A terrific woman named Kate works for me and can run the place when I'm away."

"Handy. I'm jealous."

In the morning I say to Stormy, "You want to take a road trip?"

"I had other ideas."

"I do too, but I need to drive to Great Falls."

"Breakfast out?"

"It's a date."

I unhitch the horse trailer, leaving it in the hotel parking lot with Skip's bed beneath it. I make a mental note to get some real dog food for the poor critter. She's been living on granola bars and hamburgers too much lately.

Stormy and I drive to the big city. At the idea of a real meal, my stomach begins growling. We decide to eat first, then go see Karen. Bacon, home fries, and two eggs, over easy. And very easy to get down. Everything seems unreal, being served a hot meal with real napkins. I'll have to break myself of using my sleeve.

The hospital seems sterile and hard, linoleum and shiny walls. We locate Karen's room. Her color is good and her smile even better.

"How are you holding up?" I ask her, glancing at the IV lines and monitors.

Her dark, expressive eyes have violet smudges beneath them. She's pale, but her smile is alive with her strong teeth showing white.

"Very well, compared to yesterday. It's all a blur. Sorry I didn't think about the keys earlier."

"Oh, no problem. All the women are kicking back and taking this morning to rest up."

I tell her about the arrangements I've made for her guests and how they are talking about another trip to the Wall.

Stormy says, "I'd be willing to try it again."

Her laugh is full of humor. "We'll see. Ask me again in a month."

"When are they letting you out?" I plumped her pillow.

"When I can walk. There's some talk they'll unhook me from these hoses sometime in the afternoon." Karen glances up at the IV tower. "All I want is a hot shower."

"I'll make sure you're picked up and taken to the airport." I shuffle, uncomfortable in the hospital. "Have to say, it's good to see you here. That was a rough trip for you."

"But it's over. Thanks for all you've done, Miles. And don't give me any of that 'aw shucks' stuff."

CHAPTER TWENTY-NINE

Mike, Sue, and Barbara are packed and ready to go by the time we've been to Benchmark to retrieve the van. Kamau and Luci are ready for a trip to town to drop them off at the airport.

We're all gathered at the van hugging each other. Like every group of women I'd ever traveled with, most of us are reluctant to separate. A mint green Forest Service truck pulls up next to us. A man in a green uniform gets out and comes up to the group. He takes his hat off and says, "Good afternoon, ladies. I'm from the Spotted Bear Ranger Station. I understand you are the party that just came out from the outfitter camp by White River."

I say, "Yes, that's right."

"You had to leave your pack animals up there?"

"We did. And all our gear. The fire blew up too fast to pack out, so we ran them north. We are planning to go back in to get them as soon as we're able."

"There's been a closure for all recreational purposes in that area."

"Hardly recreation to retrieve our pack animals," Stormy says, bristling.

"We've sent a plane over the pass and the extent of the burn to assess the area, but if we let you go in, we may require an escort. You know what we say, 'Life first, property second.'"

"I know those trails as well as anyone, so I can't see the need for an escort."

"Sorry. It's policy. The trails will be closed for probably two or three weeks. Not sure yet, but I may allow you in earlier. An escort will meet you in Benchmark."

"Those pack animals are going to run out of feed," I say.

He frowns sincerely. "Sorry. Do you have a contact number so we can let you know when it is safe to go in?"

I give him both Jess's and my numbers.

He is turning away when I cough and say, "There's another problem."

Alert, he turns back. "What's that?"

"There's a dead man at the bottom of the Wall."

"Oh?" He rocks back on his heels.

"We were held hostage by three men at the camp along the White River. One of them was killed and probably eaten by a bear, near the last river crossing from the west side, before the camp. You'll find any of his remains left by the bear at that location. The next morning the fire blew up and nearly caught us trying to ride over the pass, so I made the decision to go up Haystack to bare rock. It happened up there."

He frowns. "What exactly happened?"

"He had a gun and was threatening us. I tried to get it away from him, and the gun went off in the fight and shot one of our members. She's in the Great Falls hospital. In the scuffle, we rolled off the edge onto a ledge. He lost his balance and fell."

Stormy adds, "We don't know his name. The other men called him Bridger. He had saddlebags with him that held seven hundred thousand dollars. We have it here at the hotel, in the safe."

"I'm sure he stole it," I put in. "They were all desperate men."

"So, three men? Who is the third?"

"We brought him back with us. The sheriff picked him up at Benchmark. He's the one shot the DNR man in Michigan."

"Oh, yeah. We were told to be on the lookout for him. Sounds like you gals had a rough trip."

"You don't know how rough," Barbara says.

Stormy says, "One of us was raped by the one that met up with the bear."

"Has she seen a doctor?" he says. At my nod he continues, "There'll have to be an inquest."

What a can of worms.

After he leaves, Barbara, Stormy, and I just stare at each other.

Stormy says, "I'm glad Jess missed that. It's not over for her, is it?"

❖

The time with Stormy is bittersweet. She loves the ranch and is easy and wonderful with Norburt. "Now I know where you live," she tells me with a seductive smile.

Sooner than we expected, and I'd hoped, the call came from Spotted Bear that we could go in the day after tomorrow. My cousin is already lined up, and I plan on leaving Skipper at home.

Our escort turns out to be some eighteen-year-old kid. He looks his age in spite of the uniform. The ride in to the Bob took a whole lot less time with just the three of us, trotting a lot of the way. At the pass, we have our first view of the devastation. Blackened snags stand sentinel. Smoke rises, curling around with the breeze. The stink of the fire's aftermath follows us as we ride down toward the bright water, seen through the bare trees. Funny how sweet the smoke from a campfire smells, and how rank the stench of a forest fire.

When we ride into the camp, we can see we have our work cut out. All that's standing from the cook tent is the little stove. Amazingly the two tents we spent our time in are untouched. This is totally unexpected. All the women's personal gear inside the third rolled-up tent is fine, as are the packsaddles.

Half the corrals are burned, but we can still rig up enough poles to run the horses in when we round them up. If need be, we can always cut some more pole trees.

Our escort bids us a welcome good-bye. "I've got to check on the ranger station down at the mouth of the White River. I don't think you'll have any trouble on the way out."

"There was a bear down that way, but I'd guess he's long gone since the fire came up through there."

"Thanks, ma'am. I'll keep an eye out." The boy rides across the river, and soon we are alone again.

We set to work, first digging the packsaddles out from under their dirt-covered tarp. They are totally untouched. A couple of the sun showers are fine, but the rest are little mounds of melted rubber. I know we will want a shower later, so I fill the two good ones.

We spent most of the rest of the afternoon digging through the rubble of the cook tent for anything salvageable. Large piles of burnt garbage are stacked to one side. We will pack out everything we can, then notify the outfitter who rented us the place about what is left.

We finally quit scavenging, and I brew some coffee on the grill stove beside our old tent.

"Let's take our time tomorrow to get everything done," Stormy says.

"No rush." I stretch my legs out crossing my ankles. "I'm beat."

That night we curl up together under the stars, too tired to do anything but be close. We awaken with the knowledge that our time together is running out like hourglass sand.

We work hard that day, fixing the corral and packing up the women's belongings and as much of the garbage as we can condense into the panniers. Last, we strike the two tents, bundle them up, and have them ready to load by evening.

In the morning, we catch the hobbled horses and ride up toward Gladiator to round up the stock.

"They look good. Even the black mare," Stormy observes.

"Yes. Those claw marks have healed well. But the hair is growing out white. Like the bear freeze branded her."

"Jess won't like that...probably sell her. Too many memories."

This is a much harder job without Skip. They are reluctant to go back toward camp and into the after-stink of the fire. With a lot of hard riding, we finally get them headed down the trail across the White River into the corral.

The morning is bright and clear. Stormy and I get the panniers lashed on the Decker saddles with the women's gear on top. All the horses and mules are carrying something, even if it's just garbage, so by the time we're ready to ride, the place looks a lot better. As we head out of camp, I look back over my shoulder, flashing on the day we rode in, discovering the men's occupation, and all the agony that followed. Strange. It is like the fire purified the camp. Before long, wildflowers and new-growth trees will spring up.

CHAPTER THIRTY

The racket of the Core-Bond machine placing the insulation in the ceiling makes hearing who is on the telephone almost impossible.

"Rachel," she shouts.

"Bite me!" I say with fond memories of Candace.

"...want to come visit."

"Look. Let me call you back when I can hear you. Give me your number."

She does, and I repeat it a few times so I get it right.

When the guys take a lunch break, I dial her back. "Okay, now we can talk. What's this about wanting to visit?"

"I'd like to ask you out on a river date. What's the fishing like around you?"

"World class. There is, of course, the Madison, but that's crowded with drift boats and people in waders shoulder to shoulder along the bank. The Jefferson is just as good and hardly anyone fishes it. Then there's the Boulder River, which has some nice browns and rainbows. I'm sure you can cast your line someplace."

"I'm sitting here with too many great memories of our stolen hours on the White River. Do you want some company?"

"Can't tell you how much. The hay's in, and I have time on my hands until fall gather."

"So what's happening with Stormy?"

"She is happily ensconced in vet school in Pullman, Washington. I get a letter from her now and then."

"Okay, so give me directions."

I do. "Any idea when you may be blowing into town?"

"How's Tuesday sound?"

"Right. See you."

❖

Karen is back home in Maine and calls me to say she will do another trip to the Bob. Most everyone except Stormy and Roseanne will go, and she wants to know if I will, too. "I'm taking the guests at cost who were on the first trip. Doesn't seem right to charge them at all."

I think about Victoria, Jane's horse friend in Vermont, and have a flash that perhaps she would like to do this trip back to the Wall. I'll give her a call. Wouldn't hurt Karen to have a full paying guest along on the ride.

"That horror was beyond your control, but I'm sure that will be well-received. How about Jess? Will she lead the trip again?"

"She'll supply it, but she'll send two wranglers instead of coming with us."

"Too bad. I almost got to like her by the end of the excursion. So, how are you doing, Karen?"

"There's some pain still, but I led a Penobscot River trip last week, and everything went well. It's the memories that are hard to shake. If only for that reason, I'd like to do this trip. Overlay the bad with fresh experiences, you know what I mean?"

"Absolutely. I'll see if the camp will be available. Do you want the same time of year?"

"Yes. Will it be too depressing, all the burnt trees?"

"A surprising number of trees around the camp were spared. The ride down from the pass goes in and out of the burn. By the time we go in, there will be new growth, wildflowers and grass, so it won't look so stark."

"We'll check in with each other in the spring, right?"

"I'm glad you're okay, Karen. I was worried there."

"Me too."

❖

Over the next couple of days, I drive to Helena to lay in some fresh supplies and then clean house for Rachel's visit. I'm pleased she wants to fish with me. Much as I've tried, I can't seem to get any of my friends interested. There's something unbelievably companionable about wandering a river with a friend within shouting distance, someone to discuss which fly to use and admire your catch.

A part of me is guarded, aware I find her attractive in a powerful way that reaches deep within. Stormy took up just the right amount of space to get me through the awful frozen place left by Jane's death. Now my heart is open, exposed, and very vulnerable.

❖

Rachel arrives, bringing with her all her wonderful enthusiasm for life. We wander my favorite spots, catching a lot of fish, releasing most and eating some.

At dinner one night with fresh trout, she says, "Glad you're not one of those purists. Catch and release only."

"I go by the book, except if it's a cutthroat. I always release them even if that district allows you to keep them. But

I figure browns aren't native and there're a lot of rainbows, and they are very tasty."

"That Jefferson River is a well-kept secret. I have to admit, one thing I love about fly fishing is the serenity of being beside a river." Rachel sets her fork down and says, "So, what do you do with yourself, other than the ranch work?"

"Leatherwork. I build saddles and the occasional bridle. Go to town to dance. There's a group of lesbians my age that have a once-a-month potluck in Helena. I try to go just to keep in touch with my community. Have to admit it gets lonely at times."

"Yes, I can imagine. For me, too." Rachel looks out the kitchen window. "Must especially get lonely in the winter. But I've loved spending time with you, so I hope we can do it again."

"You bet." We have had a wonderful time together, talking about everything: books, music, politics, even spirituality. I can see we have been cultivating a base for intimacy, like two farmers readying the soil, finding the hardened clods, adding dark compost, and feeling the friability sifting through our fingers.

When we say good-bye, we bridge the space between us with our hands, fingers intertwined, and our eyes searching beneath skin. She hugs me with one of those "girlfriend hugs" and tries like the dickens to make it not last too long.

I watch Rachel's green Toyota RAV4 fade down the driveway, dust pluming up in its wake. With a shake, I go out to Norburt, who's cleaning the chicken house. "Everything good?"

"Sure thing, Sis."

"I'm going for a ride to check on the south fence," I tell him, slapping my thigh for Skip.

On the way to catch up Buck, I have to laugh remembering

that exchange between Jane and me about riding for pleasure. A big hollow place lurks, and I know I have to have a horse beneath me. Call it my spirituality.

But I can't just go out and wander around. Has to be some goal, or work.

I stuff the fence pliers into my saddlebags, swing my leg up across Buck's back, and ride south. Skipper lopes along beside Buck, her mouth open in the big, tongue-lolling grin of a collie. She is rested up and happy to be home again in her own bed, with her familiar companions, Myrna, Scout, and Burt. We are all Skip's herd to mind.

The black filly is out in the big pasture with Whitey. She raises her head and whinnies at me. I see she has gray mixing with the black around her eyes and muzzle. Time to give her a name. Smoke. Seems like a good handle for a gray.

I ride along the fence, half checking for loose wires or gaps.

My mind is full of Rachel. I ride out of the firs into the warmth of the sun, full on my face. A glow fills me from the warmth, then I realize it is Rachel. In no particular hurry, I ride back home, savoring the thought of her.

When I ride up to the barn, it takes a moment to realize her car is parked in the yard. She is sitting on the porch in the rocker. I toss Buck's reins over the tie-up bar and walk across the barnyard. As I approach, she stands and we come into each other's arms in a whole different way.

The first kiss ranges into unmapped territory. Unknown lips explore, hold upper lips, ending with a soft tip of tongue drawing along the edge of the opening. There is no invasion, no possession, only a discovery of one of the openings to our bodies. The exploration is performed at leisure without a hint of desperation, as though endless time stretches in front of us and standing together with lips and bellies touching is a state of being waiting for us to reach.

This encounter of our bodies holds such electric power that to carry the contact any further would turn us into pure energy, dissolving into sparks. When we part, air rushes into the space, and I feel my breath in gasps, my head dizzy.

About the Author

Franci McMahon mines her years of riding and breeding horses to write novels of suspense for even those unlucky enough to be born without the horse gene. Rounding out her life as a writer, she has four novels, many works in anthologies, stories for children and adults in national magazines, a poetry prize, and an enriching stay at Hedgebrook.

Beyond horses, Franci's life is filled with classical music, cooking, knitting, reading complex novels with a story, dancing close to a warm woman, and sitting in silence, often at Quaker meeting. These are some of her deepest pleasures. She divides her time between Montana and Tucson, Arizona.

Franci can be reached at author.mcmahon@gmail.com and on her active Facebook page.

Books Available From Bold Strokes Books

Amounting to Nothing by Karis Walsh. When mounted police officer Billie Mitchell steps in to save beautiful murder witness Merissa Karr, worlds collide on the rough city streets of Tacoma, Washington. (978-1-62639-728-6)

Becoming You by Michelle Grubb. Airlie Porter has a secret. A deep, dark, destructive secret that threatens to engulf her if she can't find the courage to face who she really is and who she really wants to be with. (978-1-62639-811-5)

Birthright by Missouri Vaun. When spies bring news that a swordswoman imprisoned in a neighboring kingdom bears the Royal mark, Princess Kathryn sets out to rescue Aiden, true heir to the Belstaff throne. (978-1-62639-485-8)

Crescent City Confidential by Aurora Rey. When romance and danger are in the air, writer Sam Torres learns the Big Easy is anything but. (978-1-62639-764-4)

Love Down Under by MJ Williamz. Wylie loves Amarina, but if Amarina isn't out, can their relationship last? (978-1-62639-726-2)

Privacy Glass by Missouri Vaun. Things heat up when Nash Wiley commandeers a limo and her best friend for a late drive out to the beach: Champagne on ice, seat belts optional, and privacy glass a must. (978-1-62639-705-7)

The Impasse by Franci McMahon. A horse-packing excursion into the Montana Wilderness becomes an adventure of terrifying proportions for Miles and ten women on an outfitter-led trip. (978-1-62639-781-1)

The Right Kind of Wrong by PJ Trebelhorn. Bartender Quinn Burke is happy with her life as a playgirl until she realizes she can't fight her feelings any longer for her best friend, bookstore owner Grace Everett. (978-1-62639-771-2)

Wishing on a Dream by Julie Cannon. Can two women change everything for the chance at love? (978-1-62639-762-0)

A Quiet Death by Cari Hunter. When the body of a young Pakistani girl is found out on the moors, the investigation leaves Detective Sanne Jensen facing an ordeal she may not survive. (978-1-62639-815-3)

Buried Heart by Laydin Michaels. When Drew Chambliss meets Cicely Jones, her buried past finds its way to the surface. Will they survive its discovery or will their chance at love turn to dust? (978-1-62639-801-6)

Escape: Exodus Book Three by Gun Brooke. Aboard the Exodus ship *Pathfinder*, President Thea Tylio still holds Caya Lindemay, a clairvoyant changer, in protective custody, which has devastating consequences endangering their relationship and the entire Exodus mission. (978-1-62639-635-7)

Genuine Gold by Ann Aptaker. New York, 1952. Outlaw Cantor Gold is thrown back into her honky-tonk Coney Island past, where crime and passion simmer in a neon glare. (978-1-62639-730-9)

Into Thin Air by Jeannie Levig. When her girlfriend disappears, Hannah Lewis discovers her world isn't as orderly as she thought it was. (978-1-62639-722-4)

Night Voice by CF Frizzell. When talk show host Sable finally acknowledges her risqué radio relationship with a mysterious caller, she welcomes a *real* relationship with local tradeswoman Riley Burke. (978-1-62639-813-9)

Raging at the Stars by Lesley Davis. When the unbelievable theories start revealing themselves as truths, can you trust in the ones who have conspired against you from the start? (978-1-62639-720-0)

She Wolf by Sheri Lewis Wohl. When the hunter becomes the hunted, more than love might be lost. (978-1-62639-741-5)

Smothered and Covered by Missouri Vaun. The last person Nash Wiley expects to bump into over a two a.m. breakfast at Waffle House is her college crush, decked out in a curve-hugging law enforcement uniform. (978-1-62639-704-0)

The Butterfly Whisperer by Lisa Moreau. Reunited after ten years, can Jordan and Sophie heal the past and rediscover love or will differing desires keep them apart? (978-1-62639-791-0)

The Devil's Due by Ali Vali. Cain and Emma Casey are awaiting the birth of their third child, but as always in Cain's world, there are new and old enemies to face in Katrina-ravaged New Orleans. (978-1-62639-591-6)

Widows of the Sun-Moon by Barbara Ann Wright. With immortality now out of their grasp, the gods of Calamity fight amongst themselves, egged on by the mad goddess they thought they'd left behind. (978-1-62639-777-4)

Arrested Hearts by Holly Stratimore. A reckless cop who hates her life and a health nut who is afraid to die might be a perfect combination for love. (978-1-62639-809-2)

Capturing Jessica by Jane Hardee. Hyperrealist sculptor Michael tries desperately to conceal the love she holds for best friend, Jess, unaware Jess's feelings for her are changing. (978-1-62639-836-8)

Counting to Zero by AJ Quinn. NSA agent Emma Thorpe and computer hacker Paxton James must learn to trust each other as they work to stop a threat clock that's rapidly counting down to zero. (978-1-62639-783-5)

Courageous Love by KC Richardson. Two women fight a devastating disease, and their own demons, while trying to fall in love. (978-1-62639-797-2)

One More Reason to Leave Orlando by Missouri Vaun. Nash Wiley thought a threesome sounded exotic and exciting, but as it turns out the reality of sleeping with two women at the same time is just really complicated. (978-1-62639-703-3)